Annwyn

and the

Owl King

by

D. B. Wales

ISBN-10: 0615846777
ISBN-13: 978-0615846774

DEDICATIONS

To Oscar, Ellie and all the animals of Nature, without whom the Earth would be a lot less magical.

To Miss Ursa, the best dog there ever was.

And to Wyatt, our beloved son.

—D.B. Wales

CONTENTS

1   Introductions and Preparations   4

2   The Owl King Celebration   23

3   Lady of Emerald Lake   43

4   Cornish's Decree   65

5   The Great Escape   80

6   Woodland Council   107

7   Midnight Encounters   135

8   Winter of Discontent   155

9   The Demons of Devilkin Mountain   198

10   The Maelstrom   244

11   A Farewell and a New Beginning   269

CHAPTER 1

Introductions and Preparations

As she flitted around her house preparing to visit her friend, Annwyn Bluebell felt the butterflies swarming in her stomach. That's strange, she thought. I'm just going to Pooka's...must be the upcoming festival. But Annwyn had every reason to be nervous, for she was to be the featured musician in the Spriggin Orchestra at the Coronation of the Owl King. Moreover, it was her first performance, and the entire village was looking to her to make this the best festival ever, especially since the crowning of a new Owl King happened only once a generation.

Though jittery, Annwyn was more than ready to make her debut. The rarest beauty in all the wood, the Spriggins regarded her as a treasure. Full of love and laughter, the daughter of Gwilyn and Llangollen Bluebell was a true nature child. Annwyn's soft features were much akin to her mother's, like delicate porcelain. Her amazing deep brown eyes, full of thought and wonder, perfectly complemented the cascades of silky, auburn curls flowing over her shoulders. But perhaps the most significant part of her appearance came in the form of the bluebell sweetly poised in her thick tresses. It was this flower that gave Annwyn her full name: Annwyn of the Bluebell Clan. In fact, the Spriggins all claimed their identities and places in society from the flowers and plants about them, and few were as highly prized as the bluebell.

But Annwyn didn't see ageless beauty when she caught a glimpse of herself in the mirror in the hallway leading to the foyer. Instead, a frazzled and slightly unkempt Spriggin looked right back at her. "EEEK! Do I really look like that?" She leaned forward for a closer inspection, hoping it was just the lighting or a trick her racing mind decided to play on her. Of course, to an outside observer, Annwyn's appearance would not have seemed diminished at all, but to a young Spriggin already attempting to fight back the quivering worms of panic squirming in her belly, she was an absolute mess. Luckily, she had an escape route, the front door, which she hastily used as a means to evade her growing discomfort.

Annwyn flung wide the large wooden door to her family's charming stone house. She stepped outside, and the sweet air produced by her mother's flower garden filled her lungs and imbued her with a sense of euphoria. She breathed deeply and let the sugary scent work its magic on her frayed nerves. Her agitation washed away in a wave of pleasure brought about by the splendor of her surroundings, and though she had seen it countless times, Annwyn had to take a moment to marvel at her mother's garden. Common knowledge held that her mother had quite the green thumb, and truth be told, her garden inspired envy in more than one Spriggin as they walked past it. And how could it not? *This* garden boasted flowers not known anywhere else in the world, shimmering with the magic of the ancient forest and singing the songs known only to flowerkind. Annwyn liked to think that sitting in the garden was like sitting on the crest of a rainbow; the feeling of floating, mingled with the colors, transported her to a place even she would consider enchanted, and words can do no justice.

But there was no time for sitting! Annwyn unlatched the gate and scampered down the cobblestone path that led to Pooka's house. She had to get there so they could prepare for their roles in the upcoming festival. The festival. No longer distracted by the garden, her thoughts turned back to the festival, making her tummy crawl with a thousand little bugs. Annwyn came to a halt.

"Oh, I just know something bad will happen. How did I ever end up in this spot?" she trembled. "Why do I have to be the one who plays for the new Owl King? I'm just not good enough, and all those people will be looking at me. Ohhh…"

Just as the world started to spin, she felt something in the folds of her dress: the wooden flute she was to play that night. She took it out of its pouch and admired its intricate, hand-carved design.

A gift from her grandfather, Tristan Bluebell, she held the flute to her lips and began to play the melody he had composed, just for her, on the day she first entered the world. The fluid sounds emanating from her flute never failed to calm her, and this time was no different. She found herself being led down the trail by the music when a single chickadee alighted on her shoulder and began singing along. With her newfound friend, she danced and twirled in the beams of warm sunshine sneaking through the forest canopy. Soon she would be at Pooka's house, the creepy-crawlies in her tummy long gone.

In fact, the creepy-crawlies, butterflies and whatever else had decided to settle in Annwyn's stomach would have beaten a hasty retreat when they heard Pooka playing his signature instrument. The *whump-whump-whump* of Pooka's drum cut short the chickadee's visit, and she darted into the woods, leaving behind a few downy feathers. "Oh, don't go little bird . . . boy, it's a wonder that there's anywhere in the forest you can't hear him drumming. For a Spriggin who hardly says anything, he sure can make a lot of noise."

The primal beat thundering from Pooka's served to remind Annwyn of her good friend, who was very shy and quiet (except, quite ironically, for the drumming of course). The consensus among the village's young maidens was he was the handsomest Spriggin, and even Annwyn couldn't argue with that. No matter where he went in Willow Hills, there was always at least one pair of longing eyes cast his way, and those eyes had plenty to see: Tall and strongly built, he had thick chestnut hair which trickled down over his brow and was unable to put a damper on the glint constantly in his crystal-blue eyes. Nestled in his hair was a sweet red rose with just a hint of chocolate, for Pooka was of the kin known as the Rose Clan. Annwyn had always wished she could wear a rose, but every time she would mention this to Pooka, he would say, "I think the bluebell is just as sweet and twice as lovely." This always caused Annwyn to blush, and even now, as she drew nearer to Pooka's, her face flushed with the familiar heat of embarrassment; she wondered if the *whump-whump-whump* she felt was from the beat of the drum or from her heart.

Sitting in the willow tree in front of his home, Pooka waited for Annwyn, his nervous energy fueling his drumming. His thoughts turned to her, and somewhat unwittingly, it increased the intensity and power of his beat. Unfortunately for his neighbors, Pooka often thought of Annwyn. He caught sight of her as she approached, and he knew then, the *whump-whump-whump* he made with his hands was really made with his heart.

Annwyn drew up to Pooka's, and abruptly, the drumming stopped. With her head no longer thumping, Annwyn let out a sweet whistle, followed by, "Pooka, where are you?"

"Up here."

Sure enough, there was Pooka, as charming a sight as ever, holding his animal-skin drum among the branches and fine cascading foliage of a large and lovely willow tree. He wore a golden speckled hat that shimmered in the sun and twice as brightly in the moonlight.

"We should hurry. Ash and Dandelion are waiting for us."

Pooka jumped down from his tree in one swift movement, drum in hand, and straightened himself up. "I'm ready."

"Well, let's go then," Annwyn chirped, hands on her hips. So, together, they made their way to collect their friends. Annwyn loved walking down the mossy covered lane perpetually surrounded by a tapestry of delicate cherry blossoms that let only peeks of sunlight sneak through and dapple the ground below. "What a wondrous day to be spent with such splendid company," she said, slipping her arm under Pooka's.

Pooka, who was reeling on the inside, answered only with a nod of his head and a muffled, "Mmmph."

"Very quiet today, young Pooka-bear," she teased, using the nickname guaranteed to fluster her bashful friend.

Pooka responded with a red face.

They turned a corner, and through the clearing at the end of the lane, they could see Dandelion Buttercup and Ash Alder playing music in the meadow they were lucky enough to have in their own backyards. Dandelion, with her playful face and glistening yellow curls full of buttercups, was enthusiastic, to say the least, and very full of life. Ash was a bit more on the peevish side, (the most polite way of saying he was usually as agreeable as a soaked cat), though his boyish looks belied a sensitivity he was loath to acknowledge. The two of them were inseparable, and he always provided a humorous contrast to the fidgety Dandelion. The scene before Annwyn and Pooka illustrated this quite well: Dandelion danced in circles, shaking her tambourine, while Ash sat cross-legged on a blanket, strumming his mandolin, head down in concentration. Just grand old chums, thought Annwyn.

In the midst of her excitement, Dandelion saw her friends in the clearing, and continued her dance of fluid swirls and twirls over to them. "I wondered when you two were going to show up. C'mon!"

Before either of them had a chance to reply, Dandelion pulled Annwyn by the arm, creating a curious chain of Spriggins since Annwyn was still attached to Pooka. Ash, like usual, waited for the fun to come to him. He sat patiently, with his olive green cap placed tightly upon a head of bristly, unkempt hair that bore more than a passing resemblance to porcupine quills. An alder tree sprig poked through his spiky locks. Dandelion, with Annwyn and Pooka in tow, rushed over to Ash.

"Dandy, there's just no stopping you once you get an idea in your head," Ash quipped. "It'd take a force of nature to slow you down."

"Some of us are just more motivated than others, lazy bones!" Dandelion shot back.

"Humph," was Ash's standard reply. Annwyn and Pooka looked on, bemused; they had seen this scene play out many times before.

Annwyn decided to get in on the fun. "Ash, sometimes you're such a stinker!" she laughed.

"Yeah, well, you'd better not be a stinker tonight. Whole forest's countin' on you," he grunted in jest. "Hope you're ready."

"Why wouldn't I be ready? Did someone say I wasn't ready?" The creepy-crawlies had returned, along with the danger of a sudden swooning. Pooka preempted a spill by slipping his arm around her waist.

"Ash Alder! Shame on you!" Dandelion interjected. "You know Annwyn's the best musician in Willow Hills, and saying things like that aren't very helpful. If anyone has to worry, it's you! Why, I've never heard a Spriggin play so many wrong notes before. Do you play your mandolin with your hands or your feet?"

Ash mumbled something, presumably unflattering, under his breath.

"Maybe we could all benefit from a little practice," Pooka said softly.

At that, he eased Annwyn to the ground, sat down on the blanket next to her, and commenced tapping a muted and mellow beat on his drum. The infectious rhythm dissolved any lingering hurt feelings, and Ash began to softly strum his antique mandolin in time. Annwyn followed on her flute, and Dandelion tinged her shiny tambourine. Soon the gang grooved and swayed to the tune filling the air. Time escaped them, and the sky began to take on the first tinges of dusk. Without a word, Annwyn rose, and soon they were on their way to the mushroom circle at the very center of the village, playing their instruments all the way.

The gang of best friends approached their destination. Just about every Spriggin in the village was there, carrying sundry items for the celebration and doing their best to avoid running into each other. Though the actual ceremony would take place in the nearby redwood Fairy Circle, this ring of mushrooms served as the central hub for any village activity. Decorations, tables, fixtures and boxes containing all sorts of supplies filled the interior. The group of friends continued their melodic march, but the din of hundreds of Spriggins, frantically preparing for the most important event in the forest, drowned them out. Undaunted, Annwyn led them to the center of the mushroom circle and into the hustle-and-bustle. Directing it all was Annwyn's mother, Gwilyn, in her usual role of village organizer.

"Let's go, Sprigs! No time to waste! We've got to get this village in tip-top shape!"

In the midst of the mushrooms, the friends ceased their playing, and Annwyn sang out with glee, "Mother, we're here. What can we do?" Before Gwilyn could even acknowledge her, Annwyn blurted out, "Oh, I can't wait to help! What fun!"

Gwilyn put a finger to her rose-petal lips, suppressing a smile as she watched her daughter's ebullience bubble up. Beloved for her kindness and wisdom, Gwilyn possessed an exquisite beauty that she had recently begun to notice in her daughter. Annwyn's boundless energy and zest for life was another common trait of the Bluebell women, and it pleased Gwilyn to no end to see her carrying on the family tradition. Yet with such a momentous task at hand, her daughter needed a little focus. "Annwyn, since you seem so eager to help, why don't you and your friends hang the beeswax candles for me?"

"Oh, if I *must*," Annwyn huffed in mock tones, causing her and her mother to smile since they both knew she particularly loved this task.

"Then no more dawdling from you, young lady. You and your friends be on your way now!" Gwilyn ordered in the best authoritative voice she could muster.

"We're sorry, Mrs. Bluebell. We didn't mean to hold things up,"

Pooka said sheepishly, his hat in his hands.

"Well, I'm feeling charitable today. Apology accepted, young man," Gwilyn responded with a slight bow of her head.

Annwyn, unable to keep up the charade any longer, burst into laughter, which had the dual effect of causing the others to laugh while turning Pooka's face into something resembling a radish.

"I think I pulled your head out of my garden this morning," Ash joked, followed by a playful poke to Pooka's ribs.

Taking pity on poor Pooka's plight, Gwilyn fixed her soft brown eyes on him and said, "Pooka, for showing virtue befitting an honorable and trustworthy young Sprig, I'm putting you in charge of the candles this year."

"Really? Me? Okay. I'll do my best, Mrs. Bluebell."

"I know you will. Well then, go and get your bundles. We can't have a festival without our candles, can we? Now, run along." She watched them go and smiled for just a moment before returning to her duties and scolding more deserving Spriggins.

Pooka found the stash of beeswax candles amid the piles of festival paraphernalia. They each took a bundle and hoisted them over their shoulders. Looking proud, Pooka made to speak, but Annwyn proved quicker: "Now, we've little time to waste. I'll take the northern section of the village. Pooka, you take the south. Dandelion, Ash, you two go east and west. How does that sound?"

"I thought I was in charge," a dejected Pooka interjected.

"You are in charge. I'm just helping you give the orders," Annwyn said with a tone that let him know resistance was futile.

No longer willing to debate the chain of command, the four friends, each with their bundles, went their separate ways and the crowds absorbed them.

Annwyn carried her candles gently under her arm, while weaving in-and-out of the bustling Sprigs, singing her favorite melody. Following the custom of all Spriggin celebrations, she lovingly placed two beeswax candles at the entrance of each cottage and lit them with the flint included in the bundle. Soon the village would be aglow with the warm light of the lit wicks. Annwyn finished her task and took a moment to admire her handiwork. Everything looks better by candlelight. The preparations neared completion, and Willow Hills looked outstanding. The Spriggins had truly outdone themselves this year. A multitude of fanciful frills festooned the village: Streamers consisting of flowers connected the houses to each other while feather-garnished wreaths adorned each doorway; polished-stone sculptures lined the walkways and accoutrements composed of leaves, mushrooms, twigs, acorns and all the other riches of the forest poked out from every corner, crevice and cranny.

As Annwyn peered about looking at all of the Spriggins engaged in readying the village, she spotted Dartmoor Nettle amongst the crowd, the one blight amid the beauty. Oh No! Eye Contact! Now she knew it was too late. Dartmoor slithered over to her, and she prepared herself for the inevitable unpleasant conversation. Dressed in his requisite dark, flowing clothing and with his sharp features, gray eyes and slicked back, shoulder-length black hair filled with protrusions of his namesake, Dartmoor had the effect of a storm cloud intruding on a sunny day every time Annwyn was forced to talk to him. The very thought of him made her skin crawl, and his particular talent was rubbing Spriggins the wrong way, like a jagged pebble running amok inside a shoe, poking, pinching and piercing at every step, and uncannily able to avoid forcible removal. Dartmoor was of the Nettle family, an arrogant and ignorant lot who were as stinging, abrasive and unpleasant as their name would suggest. Unfortunately, they also happened to be the stewards of Willow Hills.

"How are we on this splendid eve, young Miss Annwyn?" he asked unctuously.

"Fine. Thank you for inquiring, Dartmoor," Annwyn cringed, forcing a halfhearted smile. She hated to fake niceties, but unlike her present company, she tried to avoid confrontation if possible.

"No doubt you will be at the festivities tonight?"

"Of course, I'm in the orchestra. Won't you be attending?" she asked without real concern or care.

"It is my duty, as Son of the Steward, to be present. It would be an outrage for a Spriggin of my standing to miss an event of this magnitude, most surely. And since it seems we are both attending the celebration, why shouldn't we go together?"

Her jaw dropped, and her eyes widened; shocked to the point of incoherence for the first time in her life, Annwyn went mute. What could she say? What could she do? She hadn't felt this way since she accidentally disturbed a nest of yellow jackets, and at the moment, she would have preferred the yellow jackets. And all the while, Dartmoor stood there, lording over her with a smug and contented look on his face, gleeful at watching her squirm.

"Well, I'm waiting, and there are few who dare to leave me waiting."

Annwyn crossed her arms and assumed a defiant stance. "I already have plans to attend with my *friends*, Dartmoor."

He drew closer to Annwyn, causing her to back away ever so slightly. He locked his eyes with hers, and his words seeped out: "Then they'll be awfully disappointed when they find out you're going with me, won't they?"

"You've got some nerve, Nettle. I wouldn't go with you if you were the last Sprig on Earth!"

The scurrilous Spriggin poised himself to deliver an even harsher tongue-lashing, one of his favorite pastimes, when a familiar voice called out, "Ho there!" Much to Annwyn's relief, Dartmoor averted his eyes and peevishly scanned the swarm of Sprigs to identify the rapscallion who had robbed him of putting this obstreperous girl in her place. From down the lane appeared Llangollen, Annwyn's father, a beam of sunshine cutting through Dartmoor's overcast pall. Annwyn couldn't ever remember being so happy to see him, and she abruptly quit Dartmoor and rushed over to her father as he worked his way through the crowd. He was a stout, pleasant man with a jovial, ruddy face framed by silvery dreadlocks and a white, braided beard, which, in its full bloom, reached his prodigious belly. Annwyn threw her arms around his impressive frame and fiercely hugged him, halting his progress and nearly knocking the wind out of him.

"Oof! Not so tight my dear, you'll pop me like a grape!" he said with a laugh and a kiss on his daughter's cheek, which she returned.

"I'm so glad you're here!" Annwyn said, squeezing even tighter.

"My, my, I had no idea I was missed so dearly. Ha! I suppose absence makes the heart grow fonder, though it's only been a few hours since we lunched. Heh, I must say, what a pleasant surprise to see you out here talking with Dartmoor. I didn't mean to interrupt, so let me say hello, and I'll be off again."

"Let's just go, Daddy. I'm done talking to him."

"Oh, Annwyn, where are your manners? Salutations are in order, and it would be rude to leave now."

"I know, let's go."

"Annwyn Bluebell, I won't slight the Steward's Son. Why, if word got out that I comported myself in such a way, your mother would never let me live it down. Come, just a quick hello." Llangollen and Annwyn, refusing to relinquish her grasp on her father, made their way over to Dartmoor, who disguised his disgust just enough to appear to receive them favorably. He and Llangollen shook hands. "Well now, what say you, Dartmoor Nettle?"

"Sir, I was just inviting your daughter to the celebration, but I hear she has already made plans," said a suddenly crestfallen Dartmoor.

Llangollen turned a doubtful eye and raised eyebrow to his daughter. "With whom, may I ask?"

"My friends. Dandelion, Ash, Pooka, remember Daddy?"

"Annwyn, you must accept Dartmoor's proposal to attend the celebration," Llangollen said, somewhat stiffly with a suddenly hollowed-out voice.

"But father, mustn't I keep my word before accepting another *invitation*?" No way would she use the word proposal.

"You will accept Dartmoor's proposal to attend the celebration. You would do well to get used to Dartmoor and his proposals, young lady." His voice was authority, but Annwyn balked at her father's command, for he had never spoken to her like that before. He had never spoken to anyone like that before. She loosed her grip on him and stepped back, searching his face for clues. But there were no answers to be found there. This Sprig who had nurtured and cared for her all her life now looked on her like she were a stranger; no, it was worse than that -- he wasn't really looking at her, he was looking *through* her, like she weren't there at all.

"Daddy?"

Her only answer was the same vacant stare.

"Well, now that we're all of one mind, I shall leave you until tonight, my lovely Annwyn. Mr. Bluebell, thank you for your kind words. You are indeed a wise and venerable man. Fare thee well." Dartmoor bowed, flashed his sharp smile at Annwyn, and melted back into the crowd.

Annwyn was glad to see him leave, but her troubles did not follow. "Father, what did you mean by 'you would do well to get used to Dartmoor's proposals'?"

"My dear, you're of an age now that we must think about your future. I have devoted my life to taking care of you, and want nothing more than for you to find someone who will cherish you, as I have."

"Find someone? Do you mean Dartmoor?"

"And why not? He is charming, thoughtful, and you have yet to see all the wonderful things he has to offer you and our family. You are my dearest joy, Annwyn, and I love you with all my heart. I have watched you grow into a beautiful young woman, but now it is time for my little girl to start thinking of a husband."

"Husband? Where is this coming from? And you must know if I do marry, it would never be to someone like Dartmoor Nettle!"

"Come now, the Nettles are not as bad as you have concocted in your head, Annwyn, and I'm not asking you to commit to anything. I'm just asking you to enjoy the festival with Dartmoor. I'm sure you'll have a wonderful time, regardless of your company. Humor me, my dear. This old fool could never bear the thought of his daughter being unhappy." His warm eyes beaming, he kissed her lovingly on the forehead, and with a smile mostly hidden by beard, took his leave of her.

Annwyn watched her father go.

Pooka had seen the whole thing and approached Annwyn now that she was alone. He could feel her heartache. "Annwyn? Are you okay?"

"No. No, I'm not. I-I'm sorry Pooka. I was made to accept an invitation to the Owl King Festival with Dartmoor."

For a reason he did not fully understand, Annwyn began sobbing. Pooka's disappointment with Annwyn's news was supplanted by the unease he felt from her reaction to it. She'd had plenty of run-ins with Dartmoor before, so why was she so upset this time?

Without another word, he took her in his arms and held her tight. She wrapped her arms around him and felt safe. The crowd of Spriggins pulsed around them, but for the moment, they felt like the only two in the world.

CHAPTER 2

The Owl King Celebration

It was evening, and Annwyn swept down the stairs fashioned in her finest white silk dress, which shimmered and flowed over her petite frame. She wore divine wings, tinctured in many soft hues of blue. A gift from the butterflies that every Spriggin received before they could even walk, the wings gave them the ability to fly, but only on the night of a full moon. Annwyn never missed an opportunity to wear them, and they were the perfect compliment to the pure white baby's breath and bluebells intertwined among her lustrous locks. Her face was radiant, her eyes large and luminous. Her father, seated in his coziest chair in front of a fire in the den, let out a whistle.

"My little girl'll be breaking some hearts tonight," Llangollen said with a wink.

"Thanks, Daddy," Annwyn replied, giving a little twirl.

Gwilyn, standing on the landing behind Annwyn, helped place the last of the baby's breath in Annwyn's hair before hugging her.

Without the welcome distractions of the festival, Gwilyn's mind turned to what she and Llangollen had discussed earlier—Dartmoor and their daughter. Her heart was heavy, for she hated the choices they were forced to make for Annwyn. She wished she could change her daughter's path, since she knew that Annwyn did not love Dartmoor, nor would she ever, but there was nothing she could do; these events were set in motion many moons ago under circumstances she still didn't understand, though not for a lack of trying.

In the course of their conversations on the topic of the match, Llangollen was insistent, even bordering on belligerent, something a Spriggin of his mellow nature normally would not have been. This troubled Gwilyn a great deal since she could count on one hand the number of arguments she and Llangollen had over the years, and all those fights were about silly little things. She had no cause to doubt her husband, but she could never get him to reveal why the pairing of Annwyn and Dartmoor was such an imperative. In all their time together, there were never any secrets between them, so what was he hiding? Surely he didn't truly believe Dartmoor to be the ideal Spriggin for Annwyn. Who would? Yet the more she tried to find out from him, the more agitated he would become, but not with her, rather, with her questions. They confused him, even seemed to pain him as he struggled to answer them. Gwilyn always backed away when he suffered one of these bouts of distemper, since she could not bear the thought of causing him harm. What if something was really wrong with him? What if he was ill? So she coped with these terrible developments, ever holding out hope for a better future.

A loud, abrupt knock at the door shook Gwilyn from her thoughts. She answered it. "Good evening, Mrs. Bluebell. May I come in?" She dreaded that voice.

"Of course, Master Nettle," Gwilyn replied dryly.

Annwyn shivered as Dartmoor slinked his way into their house, carrying an ornate cane and bedizened in ostentatious robes and a thorny tricorn hat, which fittingly resembled horns. He stabbed his cane into the floor with a loud tap and stood there like they owed everything to him. Turning from this unpleasant sight, something caught Annwyn's eye. She noticed a slight change in her father's bearing all of a sudden; he stiffened a bit and sat upright in his chair, his eyes losing their trademark twinkle. She couldn't tell for sure, but something was just a little different about him whenever Dartmoor was around anymore. . .

"You look lovely, Mrs. Bluebell. It's not hard to tell where Annwyn gets her stunning countenance," Dartmoor grinned.

"Thank you," Gwilyn curtsied.

If it was possible, Annwyn liked him even less.

With a tip of his hat, Dartmoor turned his flattery elsewhere. "Good evening, Mr. Bluebell. Isn't it a splendid night for a celebration?"

"Indeed, it is a splendid night for a celebration," Llangollen droned, curiously rubbing the back of his neck with his hand.

"And Annwyn," he savored her name, "your beauty is certainly matchless the world over."

"Your words are very kind, Dartmoor Nettle," Annwyn offered in reply. Her eyes briefly met his before she turned her head to the side, nose ever so slightly in the air.

Then there was another loud knock at the door.

"Now, who could that be?" Gwilyn asked.

She opened the door, and with a petulant *humph!* in burst village troublemaker Rowan Blackthorn, who also held the dubious and unenviable honor of being Dartmoor's best friend. The scruffy Spriggin looked the same as usual, with his stringy hair, pointy ears, beady little eyes and curdled expression poking out from underneath his dingy brown hat. Completing the picture were tattered, unwashed overalls, a threadbare undershirt and grubby overcoat. Though most Spriggins wouldn't have worn such an outfit to wallow in a pigpen, this was Rowan's formal wear. At least he had shoes on. Ever the gracious houseguest, Rowan clapped his hands against the sleeves of his coat, fouling the air with puffs of crusty dust. After a thoroughly nauseating snort, he produced a soggy handkerchief from his pocket and spat into it, much to the chagrin of the horrified Bluebells. He replaced it and belched out, "Why'd ya keep me waitin' out there?

Ain't very neighborly of ya!"

"Welcome to our home, Rowan," Gwilyn said, tamping down her disgust.

"If you say so, sweets," he answered, scanning the area. "Ain't much ta look at if ya ask me."

"What is *he* doing here, Dartmoor?" Annwyn demanded.

"Damnation! Y'got a problem?" Rowan barked. "Such a little—"

"Settle yourself, Rowan. That is no way to speak to a lady. Annwyn, I've asked him to join us as he has no one with whom to attend the celebration. Let us not forget Rowan here lost his family long ago, and I knew someone as compassionate as you wouldn't want him to miss out on tonight's festivities in the company of friends."

"You should have asked me first, Dartmoor Nettle."

Dartmoor drew uncomfortably close: "Why my dear, I didn't suppose someone as sweet as you would mind."

"Well, I do mind." Annwyn stared back at Dartmoor, her eyes narrowing. Their wills locked in stalemate, and Rowan gave a rusty chuckle.

Clearing her throat, Gwilyn said, "We should be on our way now. We don't want to be late." With that, the Bluebell women gathered their shawls while Llangollen got out of his chair, doused the fire, and donned his topcoat. Annwyn tied the pouch containing her flute to her dress.

"Let us be off then," Dartmoor said, opening the door and gesturing with his arm outstretched.

They began their procession outside. Annwyn felt a chill when she passed Dartmoor, but she would not let him ruin her favorite night. Suddenly, she thought of seeing Pooka later, and it made her smile.

"That's more like it, Miss Annwyn."

"It is indeed, Dartmoor Nettle," she said as she blew past him.

Once in the welcoming cool of the evening, Annwyn felt her spirits rise. The scent of spice on the crisp air flooded her with memories of festival nights past, spent with her friends, laughing, dancing, making music. She deftly allowed her unwelcome escorts to pass her, and with a glance at Dartmoor walking ahead with Rowan, she wondered if she would ever share times like those with her friends again, if she would share time with Pooka like that again. She let out a sigh.

"What's the matter dear?" Gwilyn asked, touching her daughter's shoulder and surprising her a little.

"I suppose it's nothing, Mother. I was just hoping for different company tonight, a little more to my liking."

Gwilyn placed her arm around Annwyn, and they began walking.

"I know, I know. Even I'm not sure why your father seemed so insistent on young Master Nettle accompanying you to the festival. And if I'm not mistaken, you had your heart set on a certain handsome drummer, hmmm?"

"Wh-why would you say that?" she stammered, turning crimson.

"Oh, Annwyn, you put on a good show of acting so independent, but there's no hiding what's in your eyes when you see Pooka. I had that same look when I first saw your father." Annwyn's eyes rimmed with tears. "Sweetheart, you shouldn't worry so much about it. You're playing the melody for the new Owl King tonight, an honor bestowed on a Spriggin once in a generation. And I can't think of anyone more talented and worthy of such an honor. I have never been more proud of you."

Annwyn's face softened, and they embraced. "Thanks, Mother."

"Now, run along, love. I've got to find your father; he seems to have fallen behind. Where is he? Oh, Mr. Bluebell, if it weren't for that beard, we'd never find you at night!"

In the pumpkin glow afforded by the candles lighting the promenade, all the ladies could see behind them were two stark, white braids attached to a moustache. "Sorry my ladies, I'm not as quick as I used to be," Llangollen boomed as he picked up his pace to something between falling and running. He reached his wife, and they locked arms before resuming Llangollen's less-spirited pace.

With one last look at her parents together, Annwyn negotiated through the other Sprigs heading to the amphitheater and approached Dartmoor and Rowan. Head held high, she walked alongside them.

An impish grin crossed Dartmoor's face when he presented his arm for Annwyn. "Shall we?"

"I suppose we shall," she intoned, taking hold of Dartmoor's sleeve. They were off, Rowan in tow just like any obedient lap dog would be.

The candles cast a fine light over the path as the full moon crept further into the sky. Beams of moonlight pierced the forest canopy, creating pillars of silver. The forest began to wake with the first songs of the crickets and katydids, followed shortly thereafter by a refrain of tree frogs. The perfect compliment to such a sublime night was the thick, sweet scent of honeysuckle filling the air. If any night were destined to see a new Owl King crowned, it was this one.

Annwyn, arm-in-arm with Dartmoor Nettle, took only a passing notice at her surroundings. It required all her concentration just to force politeness with her odious escort. Annwyn thought back to Pooka's warm embrace as she clasped Dartmoor's sinewy forearm, and managed a smile in spite of her present company.

"I see your disposition has improved. I thought we might have to endure a joyless evening together. Surely I am not so objectionable?"

"You would never hear me say it," Annwyn offered, eyes forward.

Dartmoor suddenly stepped in front of Annwyn, forcing her off the main street and into a shadowy alleyway. He swung his cane solidly into the wall, causing Annwyn to stop cold. Rowan used his husky frame to shield them from the passersby. Nettle's face nearly met hers, and their eyes locked. In one deft motion, he spun his cane with a flick of his wrist and brought a particularly pestilent protrusion to rest on her cheek. "Trust that I never do, Miss Annwyn. I should not take it kindly."

The spike from the cane slightly stung her, but Annwyn's gaze did not waver for a moment. No amount of pain would cause her to yield. A glint of fear crossed his face, and he pulled away from her, barreling into Rowan and nearly knocking him down. He looked upon her for a final moment before regaining his composure and walking away, tapping his cane as he went.

"He knows how to put a scare in ya, don't he?" Rowan chortled. "Where's that tongue o' yers now, eh missy?"

Annwyn was happy to show him by sticking it out with an indignant *phhtbh!* for good measure.

"You'll learn to bite that before long. Dartmoor'll see to it," he spat, walking away and mumbling to himself.

Thankfully alone, Annwyn walked out from the alley and leaned against a wizened oak tree along the lane. She calmed herself and was in the process of repositioning the baby's breath in her hair when she noticed movement overhead. She caught a glimpse of feathers moments before a young, ruddy screech owl swooped onto a limb directly above her. "Nice friends you got there, Annwyn," he said, his warm, golden eyes full of mischief.

"Oscar! What are you doing here? Shouldn't you be getting ready?"

"I could ask the same of you. 'If I'm going to be the new Owl King, I can't have an unrehearsed Spriggin playing my melody. It's just not done!'" At that, they broke out into laughter as Oscar's impression of his father, King Otus, was uncanny right down to the puffed-out chest and ruffled feathers. This was but one of many excoriations Annwyn and Oscar had endured from his majesty in the weeks leading up to the festival.

"Oscar, really, what would your mother say if she knew you were out here instead of preparing for tonight?"

"She'd say, 'Why is Annwyn out with Dartmoor Nettle?'"

"If it were up to me, I wouldn't be." Annwyn's wings hummed, springing to life and carrying her up in the air until she was face-to-face with Oscar. She hovered closer and dropped her voice to a near-whisper, though the Spriggins hustling below never would have heard them: "Oscar, I think my father wants me to marry Dartmoor."

"Whaaat!??" Oscar squawked, losing a few feathers and golden eyes bulging. "That's crazy! Tell your father you've decided to marry a skunk. At least they smell better!"

Annwyn managed a laugh. "Thanks Oscar, I'm sure that'll help. But as much as I'd like to, we don't have enough time to talk about it right now. We're kinda needed at the festival. We'd better get going."

As if on cue, a drum beat echoed throughout the forest and heralded the start of the Festival of the Owl King. "Shoot! We're *definitely* not done talking about this," Oscar said. "Tell you what, when I'm king, I'll banish Dartmoor. Problem solved." Annwyn and Oscar shared a nervous giggle, which dissolved quickly under the purview of the distant, portentous drumming.

"Good luck tonight, Oscar."

"You too."

A quick embrace and Annwyn flickered to the ground and hurried down the path, dodging the other Spriggins heading to the festival. She looked over her shoulder as she ran and watched her friend disappear into the trees. A wave of warm emotions washed over her, momentarily lulling her and bringing flashes of memories she and Oscar had shared over the years. But the soporific nostalgia receded, replaced by a stark and slightly unnerving realization—the next time she saw Oscar, he would be no longer be just her friend, he would be the Owl King.

Annwyn reached the Fairy Circle of redwood trees on the outskirts of town that formed the natural amphitheater where the Spriggins and owls held the festival. She noticed Dartmoor standing impatiently at one of the ivy-covered trellises which spanned the trees and served as doorways to the circle. He did not see her, so she ducked among the other Spriggins, making her way to a separate entrance, where she slipped inside. He deserves to be stood up for being such a jerk, she thought.

Decorations of all sorts adorned the interior of the Fairy Circle. Trumpet vines, honeysuckle and ivy intermingled and threaded each tree, forming a mosaic of colors and scents along with the multitude of hanging flowers and candles. Luna moths took up residence in the vines and lined each strand, serving as both spectators and decorations, their powdery gossamer wings constantly opening and closing. Lightning bugs joined the moths among the vegetation, their pulsing, luminous lamps giving the area a slight strobe effect. Every Spriggin in Willow Hills was there, mingling and lingering, chatting and laughing on the way to their seats.

Through the bustle, it was easy for Annwyn to take her place on one of the mushrooms in the orchestra pit without being spotted by Dartmoor or Rowan. Pooka, Dandelion and Ash were already there, playing a song of celebration with the rest of the Spriggin orchestra. Annwyn untied her pouch, took out her flute, and joined them.

"Where have you been?" Dandelion snuck in between tambourine tings.

Annwyn lowered her flute. "I got held up. I'm sorry." She looked up at Pooka, but his head was down. She jumped when Pooka suddenly pounded out a thunderous roll that caused the music around him to fade until his drum dominated, growing in crescendo. He finished with a final *WHUMP* that resounded through the forest. The last of the stragglers hurried to their seats.

Everyone grew silent as the Steward of Willow Hills entered the Fairy Circle through the archway reserved just for him. The already chilly air grew colder as he imperiously swept past the rows of seated spectators.

It was Cornish Nettle, Dartmoor's father.

An imposing figure, he was much taller than the other Spriggins, and the silver runes covering his flowing black robes glistened with the light of the full moon. His narrow face, with its cruel mouth and cold eyes, caused several Spriggins to look away when he gazed upon them. His wife Glenna floated by his side, a captivating but unsettling sight in her lavish silk dress and her long black hair resplendent with nettles. Dartmoor slinked closely behind, heading a procession of ceremonial courtiers. When they reached the center, the entourage encircled Cornish, and they stepped on a platform atop a mound of moss. Cornish raised his hands, palms facing upward, and the mound grew in height, creating a pillar from the moss and placing him and his retainers above the crowd. When it reached its zenith, Cornish lowered his hands. His sharp features and piercing eyes focused intensely, and more than one Sprig felt uneasy when he spoke.

"My fellow Spriggins, tonight we gather for an occasion as ancient as our village—the crowning of the new Owl King of Anglia Forest. May he continue to protect the forest and all who inhabit it. Owls and Spriggins have spent an eternity living beside each other in peace. Let us hope the bonds we have forged with them will continue to grow stronger with each passing day. And I pledge, as your steward, that nothing will prevent our continued existence together from being a harmonious one. Now, without further ado, I present to you, King Otus and Queen Asio!"

Cornish raised both arms in the air and threw his head back. All of the Spriggins looked up to see the spectral images of hundreds of screech owls filling the sky, visible only in flashes as they passed through the moonbeams. There was a loud, collective gasp, followed by cheers of excitement, as two regal and proud owls swooped down and landed on the platform next to Cornish. After respectful bows to their hosts, Otus and Asio gazed out upon their cheering friends while the rest of the owls alighted throughout the redwood trees on the perimeter of the Fairy Circle.

"My friends," King Otus began, "you honor us with your welcome. Tonight we witness the end of my rule as the keeper of balance in Anglia Forest. I have watched Willow Hills for many years, and of all the places in the wood, it is certainly the most precious.

When I think of all the happiness we have shared together, all the troubles we have overcome together, I cannot help but feel a little sad with the knowledge that I will no longer be the one to protect the greatest friends owlkind have ever known. But let us speak no more of an old owl's sadness. Tonight is a night of great joy! Tonight, Asio and I crown our son Oscar, King."

That was Annwyn's cue. She alone stood on top of her mushroom and began playing her flute. A sweet melody poured forth and coaxed the new Owl King down from his perch; Oscar swooped down and circled above the crowd, as if floating on the notes rising from Annwyn's flute. Heeding the slowing tempo, Oscar glided to the platform, his landing accompanied by the last dulcet tones in the air. He turned and faced his parents.

Otus removed the crown from his head and held it over his son's. The assembly was held rapt by what they saw. The crown shone in the moonlight, its interwoven bands of platinum twinkling with a celestial radiance brighter than any star. But the adorning jewels proved to be the most captivating sight. There were four of them, two on each side, and each a distinct color with its own significance: The aquamarine gathered the energies from the sea; the sapphire hummed with the vibrancy of the earth; the ruby blazed warmly like the sun; and the diamond whispered in the secret language of the wind. They each glowed with the power stirring in them. Yet for all its majesty, the crown was not without flaw. In the center was an empty setting where a fifth stone once rested. Mystery shrouded the whereabouts of the missing jewel to such a degree, that no one even knew what kind of treasure completed the crown. Many myths and legends sprung up over the years to explain its absence, but no one could say if they were true. Nevertheless, this magnificent crown bound all living things in the forest, protecting them against sorrow and wickedness.

"With this crown, I hereby name you Oscar, King of the Owls and the Protector of Anglia Forest!" Otus placed the platinum crown on Oscar's head, and the new king turned about for the entire crowd to see. Cries of *Hail King Oscar!* and *Long Live the King!* greeted him. Oscar spread his wings, and the owls left their roosts in the redwoods to fly down and circle around their new leader on the platform. Oscar shot Annwyn a wink, which she returned with a smile.

"Friends," Oscar began, "thank you for your warm reception. Who knew it would take me becoming Owl King to get one?" The audience chuckled. Otus put his wing around Asio, and they beamed at their son. "I know you have loved and respected my parents for decades now. I have too. They brought a prevailing peace to Anglia, for their rule was virtuous and kind-hearted, just as they are. Please know I will continue to nurture the bonds we share, so our years together continue to be fruitful. And speaking of fruit, I thought this was a party. Where's all the celebrating? I hope I didn't preen myself for nothing!"

On a wave of cheers, laughter and applause, Spriggins began

launching into the air, their wings buzzing to join the tapestry of owls, Luna moths and lightning bugs filling the night sky. Pooka beat away on his drum, creating a driving *bum-bada-bum-bum*. Ash strummed bright chords on his mandolin, and Dandelion tapped her tambourine in time. The rest of the orchestra added harps, fiddles, horns and cymbals to the already lively music.

Everyone flew by the dais to greet the new Owl King. Upon their introductions, the Spriggins noticed how handsome Oscar was with his neatly preened feathers on full display. A frill of reddish-brown fluff framed his face and highlighted his pointy ear tufts. However, most impressive were his exquisite, golden eyes: They shone with a kindness and compassion, captivating everyone who looked into them. But now, mischief entered those eyes when they noticed Annwyn rising into the air, still playing her flute.

"Excuse me," Oscar said, politely hopping from the platform and taking off after his friend, leaving a few exasperated Spriggins behind him. Some of the greeters were a bit miffed at what they considered to be un-kingly behavior, but to those who knew him, it would have been a surprise had he spent the whole evening attending his duties.

Annwyn fluttered amongst the Luna moths and lightning bugs, unaware of her approaching friend. She almost dropped her flute when Oscar zipped past her shouting, "You never could catch me Annwyn!" Not one to back down from a challenge, Annwyn chased after Oscar, higher and higher, while dodging ancient limbs and revelers alike.

"Oscar, slow down! I can barely keep up!" laughed Annwyn, almost in hysterics from all the excitement.

"Not a chance! Ha-ha!"

In fact, they were all merry. Spriggins and owls were eating, singing, dancing, and some were even sampling the sweet nectar wine. The creatures of the night speckled the sky, Spriggins amongst them, flitting, darting and dashing under the moon. The Spriggin Orchestra's spirited music heightened everyone's enjoyment. Anglia had known joy many times in all its years of existence, but few nights could compare with this one. The camaraderie felt by the merrymakers grew so intense, it heated the air around them with sultry ambiance, a wonderful alchemy transmuting the chilled night into a warm eve. At this moment, the forest kin were one.

But the beatitude died when suddenly all the lights in the forest extinguished, as if a black shroud had been thrown over Anglia. The music died, and the forest remained painfully silent for a moment. Spriggins pawed at the inky atmosphere, groping for the slightest touch of something -- a mushroom, a tree, another Sprig, anything -- which would help them make sense of the situation and regain their bearings. Even the owls, usually adept at navigating through pitch-black nights, struggled to gain perches among the redwoods. And try as they might, the lightning bugs found themselves unable to produce a glow against the unnatural darkness. The warmth that had pervaded the Fairy Circle dissipated rapidly, leaving the Sprigs and owls suddenly shivering through puffs of cold breath while the insects struggled to find places to roost and conserve heat. The first confused mumbles ceased when, from somewhere deep in the forest, something terrible whipped through the trees with a hissing wisp, carving out a path of terror behind it. Everyone held still out of morbid dread, too afraid even to breathe, let alone speak. The awful sound grew so loud that it vibrated inside everyone's heads with such intensity it threatened to burst their tympanum like overripe fruit, sending the assembled masses scrambling to cover their ears. Whatever it was emitted a banshee wail as it found its mark and plunged into it with a sickening thud.

Oscar's scream split the night.

Annwyn's blood ran cold. Even though there was no light, she alone could somehow see Oscar through the darkness. He hung in mid-air for a brief moment before he went limp and plummeted to the ground with a heavy *THUMP*. Annwyn bolted to the aid of her friend. She knelt down, wrapped her arms around him, and clutched him to her chest. His breathing was shallow and rapid, and she could feel him struggling to stay alive.

"Oscar!" she cried. No answer. She caught a glint from the crown lying on the ground, just a few feet away from them. If she could get the crown back on his head, then surely its healing powers could revive him. Annwyn released one arm and picked up the crown.

A beam of light cut through the darkness and shone upon her. It was Dartmoor who cast it from the crystal on the top of his cane. "What have you done? What have you done to our new Owl King?"

"Nothing! I-I didn't do anything!"

"Why are you holding that?" Dartmoor snarled. Light returned to the forest, and all eyes fell upon the crown in Annwyn's left hand. "You know it is forbidden for any Spriggin to touch the crown!"

Rowan Blackthorn stepped out from the shadows. "She must want it fer herself! I knew them Bluebells was wicked! She musta killed the King! Annwyn's killed the King and taken the crown fer herself!"

"I didn't, I-I would never. . ." A torrent of shouts and insults grew as Blackthorn continued his harangue and drowned out Annwyn's pleas of innocence. Everyone had begun closing in on her, accusing her, saying such terrible things. Where was her family? Where were her friends? Where was Pooka? "Please, I didn't kill him! He's not dead! Please listen!" she cried out, but to no avail.

Realizing the hopelessness of her situation, her eyes filled with tears -- no one was coming to her rescue. Unable to defend herself against the advancing mob and fearing for her very life, she stole away into the night, carrying the lifeless form of the Owl King.

CHAPTER 3

Lady of Emerald Lake

Tears streaming down her cheeks, Annwyn struggled for breath amid her sobs as she raced down the long, dark wooded path; though her body ached from carrying Oscar, the true burden came from her soul, which now wallowed in abject despair and threatened to bring her down in the darkness. On the verge of collapse, she broke free of the forest and lunged onto the soft sands at the edge of the Emerald Lake, staggering forward on wobbly legs that finally gave out, dropping her to her knees. The depleted Sprig nearly crumpled over with exhaustion, but her love for Oscar gave her just enough strength to keep her upright.

As her breathing slowed and her tears dried, Annwyn's fuzzy vision sharpened somewhat, and she took in her surroundings, hoping to get a better grasp of the situation. Normally, Annwyn wouldn't have come here, nor would have any other Spriggin. In the distant past, it was said to have been a beautiful sheet of blue, but then something strange occurred: an oppressive, dense fog slithered down from the mountains and settled over the lake, claiming the area as its own and transforming the once sparkling waters into a murky green. Since then, this place struck fear in the hearts of all who ventured too close to its shrouded, gloomy shores, but Annwyn was desperate, and she knew no one would be looking for them here.

Still clutching onto her injured friend, Annwyn calmed herself by repeating, "Believe everything will be okay, believe everything will be okay. . ." Her mind cleared, and she focused on what she needed. Gently laying Oscar in the powdery sand, Annwyn found she couldn't bring herself to look upon his wound. On the mad dash through the woods, she caught sight of Oscar's left eye in the half-light, and it horrified her. It was bad, yet she knew what would heal it. Annwyn seated herself next to Oscar, crossing her legs and resting her open palms on her knees. She closed her eyes and hummed—from somewhere in the forest, something hummed back. She opened her eyes and perceived a faint glow among the trees. She stood and walked toward the light, its brightness opening a path to her through the dense wood. There, in a small clearing, sat a moon plant patch, the stamens of each milky flower glowing like a thousand little candles in flux with Annwyn's humming. She knelt down and thanked the plant for its life before she yanked at its base and unearthed it from the soil.

Annwyn rushed back to Oscar. She carefully stripped the roots from the plant and crushed them between two rocks she had picked up. Adding water from the lake, she made a paste from the root powder and applied the unguent to the small owl's left eye before bandaging his head with the leaves of the moon plant.

"Oscar," Annwyn pleaded, trying to revive the still-unconscious Owl King, "this is all I can do for you, please wake up." He didn't stir at all, so she brought him to the lake's edge and filled her cupped hands with water, which she sprinkled on his face. There was still no sign of life in him. She let out an anguished sigh, and the force of her breath blew away a small patch of the fog. Annwyn caught a glimpse of herself in the surprisingly limpid waters of the Emerald Lake, and she didn't recognize the disheveled Spriggin looking back at her. Her mind raced. *What am I going to do? He's not waking up, and they all think I killed him. But why? Why did they turn on me? I was just trying to help him. Anyone could see that!*

"Oh, Oscar, please don't die." She began sobbing again, and her tears dripped into the lake, sending rolling ripples across its glassy surface.

Suddenly, the fog around Annwyn started swirling. In an instant, it recoiled, exposing the surface of the water in front of her. Then, the fog got thicker and formed the silhouette of a person while it grew incandescent, radiating forth an emerald light. Annwyn panicked, fell back in the sand, and scrambled to protect Oscar. Frantically, she untied her shawl and covered him with it. She tucked the precious bundle behind her and made to hide him with her wings, but they were gone, no doubt shorn from her as she bolted through the woods. Panic again surged through her body, making her head swim. Nevertheless, she sat up and assumed her most imposing, protective stance, doing her best to obscure Oscar from whatever was coming. She hoped this approaching apparition would back away at the sight of her, but the slight quiver in her voice as she spoke was less than intimidating.

"Wh-who's there? Don't come any closer! I'm warning you!"

As if in response, the luminescent green haze flared with intensity, and it blinded Annwyn for a moment. Dropping her arm from her eyes as the glare subsided, Annwyn beheld an exquisite creature, hovering just above the water, resplendent in an ethereal, white dress and having long, flowing, golden locks adorned with a shimmering emerald crown. The figure floated toward Annwyn.

"I am Emmlen, Lady of Emerald Lake. Who is this who sheds tears on my shore?"

"I'm Annwyn," she sniffled. "I'm sorry if I disturbed you. I don't want to cause any trouble, so I'll be going now."

"If you feel that's best, but I must know: What makes you cry with such a sorrowful soul?" Something in Emmlen's manner set Annwyn at ease; she lifted her wings and produced Oscar from behind her back, holding him close for a second and then laying him down in the sand. "I see. You carry a heavy burden indeed, Annwyn."

"This is Oscar, and he is the Owl King. I don't know what happened, but everyone thinks I killed him. But I didn't, I could never . . ."

"I know you did not do this, Annwyn Bluebell, though the one who committed this foul act has shrouded the truth with an evil magic. You despair, yet all is not lost. Perhaps I might tend to him?"

Emmlen glided over to Oscar, received him from a hesitant Annwyn, and tucked him into her arm. She removed her necklace with a wave of her hand, then grasped the crystal at its center and held it over Oscar's head. Emmlen began chanting in a language Annwyn did not understand, and the mist surrounding the water fairy enveloped both she and the Owl King. An intense light shone from the inside of the haze as the chanting grew louder and louder, the words of an ancient tongue echoing throughout the wood. The sound was unbearable. Annwyn fell back in the sand, covering her ears and shutting her eyes as tightly as she could. Then it all stopped. She regained her senses and knelt forward, peering into the mist, which had taken on its previous muted luster.

The fog dissipated and Emmlen lowered Oscar back into Annwyn's waiting arms. Oscar was still motionless, but his body was no longer cold, and he was breathing regularly. She looked into Emmlen's eyes.

"Will he be okay?"

"Yes, he will survive. Though his life energy is strong, he nearly succumbed to the poison."

"Poison? What poison?!"

"Whoever struck down the Owl King did so with the intention of killing him. Your dressing helped slow the venom born of hatred, a dark and evil magic even I have not seen in millennia. I have purged him of what remained, but young Oscar will never regain the use of his eye. Yet, do not lament, Annwyn Bluebell. Come with me, I shall take you to my palace, and there you both will spend the night."

Emmlen turned from them, and whispering another arcane incantation, summoned a golden boat, which materialized out of the mists and crept silently to shore. The long and ornate dhow struck Annwyn as resembling a slender sea serpent in a state of repose, hovering on the water's surface, its impressive form culminating in a sleek head. Annwyn had spent many candlelit nights in her family's study delighting in scaring herself by poring over the pages on these serpents in one of her books about the Great Waters; but unlike the oft-horrific illustrations in those books, which invariably later plagued her dreams, this stylized serpent did not inspire fear in her. Indeed, for some reason, its mere presence assuaged her and set her at ease. On its own, the ship delicately unfurled a ramp onto the sand for its passengers. Emmlen ceased her chanting.

"Please, come with me."

Annwyn climbed aboard the shimmering vessel and sat down on a cushioned bench, taking great care to keep Oscar safe next to her. Emmlen took her place at the helm, and in a fluid choreography of nuanced hand gestures, she magically turned the dhow to face the shrouded, open waters of the Emerald Lake. But instead of the boat gliding forward, its curved prow began to sink. They were going down! Annwyn sucked in a last, desperate gulp of air and clutched Oscar close, closing her eyes and waiting for the icy waters to wash over them. Yet that didn't happen. Annwyn built up the courage to peek through one eye and soon was staring, aghast at what she saw. She beheld the underwater world of the Emerald Lake just as clearly as she would an open meadow on a sunny day. Fish and turtles darted this way and that through the azure atmosphere as though they were birds in the sky. To Annwyn's wonderment, the water rushing past her felt like nothing more than a warm breeze.

They continued on this way until Emmlen steered them to the edge of a ridge, and they dropped down into a seemingly infinite abyss. Annwyn felt panic rising, but it was extinguished when she noticed lights flickering in the distance. As they drew closer, the darkness melted away, and Annwyn could make out thousands of tiny creatures glowing from within, illuminating the way to the Emerald Palace, which grew imposingly larger the nearer they drew. The immense structure sat on a vast plain of sand, its many spires pulsing with the same ethereal glow as the creatures surrounding it; the energy flowed through the entire palace, causing its crystalline walls to twinkle.

"I've never seen anything so breathtaking in all my life," Annwyn gasped, bubbles trickling from the corners of her mouth.

"You are privileged, young Bluebell. There are few who have ever lain eyes upon my palace. Here you will be safe until you are ready for what awaits you."

"How do you know my last name? I've not mentioned it once this whole time."

"We have arrived," Emmlen intoned as a jade portcullis lifted. Breaking the water's surface, they entered an arched tunnel that opened into a cavernous bay. The luminescent lichen growing all over the polished marble walls and ceiling gave off an ambient light, which danced wildly with the reflective flares, born of the water below, flailing across the rounded contours of the expansive chamber. Annwyn didn't have time to wonder how she emerged from the water dry and warm, for the complex, dazzling beauty of this place left her with eyes wide and mouth agape. On the smooth stone pier stood three water fairies adorned in silver robes and awaiting the arrival of their Lady. Emmlen guided the boat to them, and they docked.

"Lady Emmlen, we have readied the rooms," said Fein, the fairy with blue eyes.

"Well done. Flax, take Oscar to his quarters. And Fern, escort Annwyn to hers."

"Yes, milady," they replied in unison.

Flax reached his arms out, and Annwyn reluctantly handed Oscar over to him. Flax cradled the bandaged and bundled owl while Fern helped Annwyn onto the dock. "Please, follow me," Fern said with a bow.

Fern turned and Annwyn started off with her, but she glanced over her shoulder and saw Flax carrying the owl to the archway at the opposite end of the dock. "Where is he taking Oscar?" Annwyn piped up, voice tinged with panic.

"He needs to heal still, young Bluebell," Emmlen said, walking toward Annwyn. "He will not be far from you and will be quite safe. Now, I think it best that you retire to your room and rest. Much has happened, and you are weary. Trust me, you will see your friend when he wakes."

Her words soothed Annwyn. "I suppose I could use a nap," Annwyn managed a wan smile. "Thank you, Emmlen." The water fairy graciously bowed her head. Annwyn turned to the waiting Fern, and they walked through the archway leading to the guest chambers. Fein met Emmlen, and they turned to follow Flax and Oscar.

"Milady," Fein began, "I know you have the gift of prophesy and have foreseen these events, but do you think it wise to concern ourselves with such matters? We have never done so in the past. We risk exposure."

"There is more at stake here than you realize, Fein. I cannot help but involve myself in the Fates this time. Should Annwyn Bluebell fail, the world will fall into shadow."

They spoke no more and moved quickly through the archway.

Oscar woke on a bed of moss. He struggled to gain his footing, and after a few awkward fumblings, he regained his balance. Through blurred vision, he could make out what seemed to be a dense forest, but something was wrong. There was something on his head, covering his eye! He frantically flailed his wings in an attempt to pull the bandage off, but succeeded only in toppling himself and landing with a loud *THUD* back onto the moss. Dazed, he looked up and saw someone standing among the trees.

"Annwyn, is that you? What's going on?" Oscar squinted. "Wait a second, you're not Annwyn . . ."

"No, I am not. I am Emmlen, Lady of the Emerald Lake, and you are my guest here."

"Where's here? What's wrong with my eye? Where's Annwyn? What am I doing here?" Oscar asked with increasing speed.

"All will be answered in due course, young Owl King. For now, know your dear Annwyn is safe here with us, and it was she who rescued you, using her knowledge of the forest healing herbs." Emmlen let this sink in, and she then gestured to their surroundings. "Let not the forest deceive you, for you are indeed in the Emerald Palace, far below the waters of the lake. To speed the healing process, this chamber becomes the environment best suited for recovery of the ill and wounded. In your case, a dense wood much like Anglia."

"Emerald Palace, huh? Never heard of it."

"And yet here you are, Owl King. Things do not exist based solely on your knowledge of them."

"I guess not. What about my eye?" Oscar asked hesitantly.

"What do you remember about last night?"

"Well, I remember . . . the festival, being crowned. I remember my mom and dad, all of my friends, everyone singing and dancing. I remember teasing Annwyn and her chasing me through the trees until it went black. I felt a great pain... and then I woke up here."

"The pain you felt was from an evil magic. Someone conjured an incubus from the Nether Realms to kill you, Owl King, and though Annwyn and I saved your life, we could not save your eye."

"You mean I'm blinded?"

"Yes, I'm afraid so. Unfortunately, you will carry this wound the rest of your days."

"Who did this? Who did this to me?"

"The answer is shrouded in darkness. Even I cannot see through it, and many suspect your dear Annwyn is the culprit."

"Annwyn? That's crazy! She won't even swat at flies! She couldn't do anything like this!"

"Nor would she ever."

Oscar hopped to his feet. "Then we need to go back to Willow Hills and tell them she didn't do it!"

"No, Owl King, you cannot yet return there. I sense many minds already poisoned against Annwyn. Should she go back, the same evil that claimed your eye could claim her life. Besides, though you have been named Owl King, you are without your crown and therefore, your powers greatly diminished."

"Any chance you know where it is?"

Emmlen lowered her head.

"So, it's all good news then…well, what do we do?"

"For now, you will rest. You have woken to a different world, but you are not yet ready to meet it. Once you are healed, I shall reveal your path."

"What about Annwyn?"

"Your destinies are intertwined. You will need her strength, and she, yours, before all can be set right again in Anglia Forest. This is much for you to bear, but take heart young king, you will not be alone. Your trials will be great, but none so that you cannot overcome them with help. Now, I shall take my leave and allow you to find sanctuary here."

"I suppose you're right. Thank you, Emmlen."

"Sleep well, Owl King." Emmlen vanished among the trees, and Oscar found himself alone, wondering if he would ever rest again.

Fern knocked on Annwyn's chamber door and promptly let herself in. She found a groggy Annwyn already resting on her elbows underneath her blankets. "Did you sleep well, Annwyn Bluebell?"

Annwyn yawned and rubbed her eyes. "Mmm, yes, very well, thank you."

"Milady sent me to inform you that your presence is requested in the dining hall. A feast has been prepared in honor of you and the Owl King."

Annwyn shot up in bed. "Oscar? Is he okay?"

"You will see for yourself at the feast."

"Oh right, the feast." Annwyn's belly grumbled. "Well, now that you mention it, I am kinda hungry."

"Then let us go."

Annwyn threw aside her covers, got out of bed, gave a good

stretch, and followed Fern out of the room. They entered a cloister, one side of which was comprised entirely of windows. The glow from the effulgent creatures swimming outside the glass provided the primary light source, though it constantly flickered with their rhythmic movements. Temporarily transfixed by this underwater ballet, Annwyn found it no small task to keep pace with Fern.

"Hey Fern, what're all those underwater lights out there? They look like they're alive."

Fern kept walking with nary an acknowledgment.

"Helloo, Fern?"

Again, nothing.

Annwyn proved she could take a hint and followed her mute chaperone down the hall. They turned the corner, passed through a foyer, and walked into the opulent dining hall. It had high, vaulted ceilings, and its walls contained dozens of stained glass windows, illuminating the room by leaving it awash in pulsing beams of colored light. Annwyn took a moment to gaze around the room when her eyes fell on a most welcome sight: There at the head of the long, wooden table sat Oscar, already well at work on a plate of crispy crickets and katydids.

"Oscar!!!" she cried out. In a flash, she ran over to him and scooped him up, mid-cricket. "I'm so happy to see you!"

"Mmph, me too," Oscar muffled through a mouthful. He finally had a chance to swallow and hugged Annwyn back. "I'm happy to see you, as long as you stay on my right." He gestured to his eye patch.

Annwyn's head drooped precipitously. "I'm sorry about your eye, Oscar. I tried to help, I should have done more."

"Don't be silly, Annwyn. Emmlen told me all about what you did," Oscar glanced at their seated hostess, "and it sounds like I owe you my life. You'll have to show me that little moon plant trick someday." He winked his good eye.

"It was nothing," Annwyn blushed. "Hey, where's your crown? I thought I had it with me up on land!" Annwyn shot a panicked look at Emmlen.

"I'm afraid the crown is lost. I sent Fein to the surface to search for it, but he found nothing."

"Oh no, how could I have done that? I'm so clumsy sometimes...I guess I dropped it. I'm so sorry, Oscar, I didn't mean to."

"Hey, I lost my crown and my eye, but at least this one still works, so one-outta-three ain't bad." He draped his wings around Annwyn in a hug, and they both smiled.

She pulled away and patted herself down. "Oh no, my flute! I don't have it!" she cried.

"Calm yourself, Annwyn," Emmlen smiled sweetly. "We found it on the banks of the lake. It awaits you, along with fresh clothing, in your room." Annwyn let out a huge sigh, much to Emmlen's delight. "Won't you please be seated and enjoy this repast?"

Annwyn sat and beheld all of the most scrumptious foods before her: blueberry and walnut cakes with honey, spicy mushroom soup with dandelion greens, cream-topped pumpkin puffs, mixed-berry tarts, butternut squash and banana nut breads, and every kind of delectable fruit pie imaginable including May apple, her favorite. Mouth watering, Annwyn plopped herself down next to Oscar, who had already resumed crunching his crispy critters, and helped herself to a generous portion of everything. They feasted and laughed, and were able to forget their recent misfortunes, if only for a while.

Stomach full and eyelids already growing heavy, Oscar rose from his place at the table. He stretched out his wings, and one leg, in a balancing act that looked like it could go wrong at any minute.

"Phew, I need a nap after a meal like that! *Buuurp.*"

"Nice Oscar, real classy," Annwyn joshed.

"Excuse me, I guess a couple crickets are still kickin'." They all shared a laugh.

"Young Owl King, you bring joy to this table, and I thank you for it. It has been a long time since these halls knew anything but sorrow. But I am afraid we must cut our merriment short, for you need your rest. Your eye still needs time to heal."

"Uh, okay. Well, I guess that's my cue. Good night then, Emmlen, and thanks for everything, especially supper."

"You are quite welcome."

Oscar turned to Annwyn, and putting on his most ridiculously regal voice, he pronounced, "And good night to you, Annwyn Bluebell, fairest maiden on this side of the table."

Annwyn giggled but composed herself enough to respond in kind, "Rest thee well King Oscar, ye of few manners."

"Some are better than none!" Oscar teased, gesturing at Annwyn with a wing and prompting another round of chuckles. "I hate to leave such agreeable company, but I'd better be off, good night." He attempted a take-off, but all he accomplished was a display of flailing wings and ruffled feathers. "Whoa, that's not good. Uh, Emmlen, could I get some help?"

"Of course." Emmlen gestured with her right hand, bringing Fern and Flax into the hall. They carried a mossy bed framed by bamboo poles.

Oscar climbed up and nestled in. "Whoo, king-size. I could get used to this. Good night again." Fern and Flax transported him and his grin out of the room.

Emmlen smiled and turned to Annwyn, "Shall we take a walk? We have much to discuss."

"Okay, I guess we do have a couple of things to talk about."

Annwyn rose and followed Emmlen out of the dining hall and into the hallway, which was lined with large windows that offered a spectacular view of the underwater world lit by the darting beasties. Annwyn could not help but stop for a moment to marvel. "It's like looking into a dream. I never would have imagined all of this was down here."

"There is much in this world that is hidden from sight." Emmlen paused and looked out into the luminous depths. "No matter how magnificent or mundane, sometimes things escape our notice when they should have our full attention." They began walking again. "The waters enclosing this palace were once known as the Azure Pool until the wisps of viridian fog covered its surface with gloom and infused it with its hue. But the crystal waters never lost their sparkle, causing you Spriggins to rename it the Emerald Lake."

"Why did the fog come to the lake?"

"Here we are."

Emmlen led Annwyn into a grand gallery lined with two colonnades, each column supporting a torch, giving the room a warm glow. In between the pillars stood marble statues depicting fabled fairies adorned in long robes. Some held tomes of wisdom, some musical instruments, and still others struck more imposing stances wielding swords and maces. They walked among them all, an awestruck Annwyn taking time at each one to read the inscriptions at their bases and to escape momentarily into realms of adventure, peril and mystery.

"Who are they, Emmlen?"

Each one of these statues stands testament to a fairy who, in ages past, rose to meet a challenge thought to be all but insurmountable. Their deeds of heroism used to inspire courage where there was once fear, but the world above has long since forgotten them. Now they rest here, waiting for the time when their stories can once again be known."

Annwyn stopped at an empty pedestal. "There's no statue here."

"No, there is not, for the story of that hero has yet to be told. Once that tale has passed into history, its monument will complete my hall, and my palace, allowing it to return to its former glory."

"Former glory? What do y—" Annwyn turned around and found Emmlen holding a ring radiating green light in her outstretched palm. It was the most wondrous thing Annwyn had ever seen; the runes on its thin silver band pulsed in unison with the energy exuding from the main setting of diamonds and emeralds arranged in the shape of a flower. Entranced by the ring, Annwyn hesitantly extended her hand, meaning to touch it.

"You may take it, for this is yours, Annwyn Bluebell."

"Mine? I don't ever remember owning this. How do you know it belongs to me?"

"Because it always has been in your family. Long ago, the Matriarch of the Bluebell Clan wore this ring, and she intended it to be passed down through the generations. But that was before a great evil stirred and threatened to destroy Anglia. Her attempts to thwart it failed, and she feared this malevolent force might corrupt the ring. She entrusted it to me, and I brought it here until such a time it could be placed back on the hand of a Bluebell."

"But why me? Why not my mother or my grandmother? What have I done to deserve this?"

"The will of the Fates is not always easily discerned, Annwyn Bluebell. Know that you are meant to have this ring." Emmlen held it forth.

Annwyn delicately took the ring and put it on. It fit as though it had been made for her finger.

"The evil that once menaced Anglia has returned. It now consumes your village, and soon it will grow, encompassing all that live in the forest. If it is not stopped, it will blanket all of existence, blotting out the sun, sapping the warmth from the land and plunging the world into eternal darkness. You must use the Emerald Flower ring to fight this scourge."

"Fight a scourge? I can't fight any scourge. I need to get Oscar back to the village!"

"You mustn't go back there, for danger awaits your return. Your destiny lies on a different path now. Use the Emerald Flower to find your way, and in turn, its power will guide you through your darkest times and blackest moments."

"How do I use the ring then? I mean, what does it do?"

"It has many abilities, not all of them known to me. It was this ring that brought the fog and concealed my palace beneath this lake, so be mindful of its potency. But when the time comes, you will know how to wield it, you've always known."

"I just don't understand."

I know this may be hard to grasp, but you must. For there is more."

"More? How can there be more?" Annwyn looked up from the ring, and her voice grew soberly fragile: "I'm not sure I can handle all this."

"You are not the first to doubt her fortitude when faced with a terrible challenge. Understand you have a great strength not yet realized. It is this inner virtue which will guide you to something that legends speak of, the Moonstone."

"Moonstone? I didn't even think that was real."

"What do you know about it?"

"I heard stories about it when I was growing up. We'd tell them when we had our autumn bonfires. Mostly they were about the monster guarding the stone, so I always figured they were like ghost stories, meant to scare the kids into being good. You know, 'if you go out after dark, the monster'll get you'."

"Indeed."

"None of that's true, is it?" Annwyn's voice quivered again.

"Like any story, it has traces of truth. You will find out for yourself soon enough which parts are real. But come what may, you must use the Emerald Flower to seek out the Moonstone. Only if you possess it, can you hope to wrest the grip of evil from this land."

"What about Oscar? I won't leave him."

"Nor will you. The two of you share a bond far greater than even you can imagine. Tomorrow, you will set forth on your journey together to confront this evil. Find the Moonstone, and the rest will be revealed to you. Now, I must away to tend to other matters. I trust you will be able to find your way to your chambers?"

"Yeah, sure, I'll be okay. Good night, Emmlen."

"Good night, Annwyn Bluebell." She disappeared down the hall.

Annwyn, alone, basked in the glowing marvel of the Emerald Flower. The shadow she cast seemed longer for some reason.

CHAPTER 4

Cornish's Decree

Chaos reigned in Willow Hills. The world had gone dark and then, the unthinkable: Annwyn Bluebell killed the Owl King and stole his crown. Dartmoor's insinuations and Rowan's outright incriminations precluded any other conclusion—she must have done it. *But hadn't her face been ashen? Hadn't she cried at the sight of Oscar? Annwyn couldn't have done this!* These first few cries of disbelief gave way to the roar of accusations led by Rowan Blackthorn, and soon the amphitheater swelled with a sea of raised fists and brandished talons. Here and there, level heads tried to bring calm to the throng, but they were no match for the enflamed passions burning in their hearts. After Annwyn disappeared with Oscar and the crown into the woods, the debate was over. These two forest peoples, who had been joined in harmonious celebration just moments ago, now turned on each other with a frightening ferocity.

"Annwyn did this! She killed our king!" shouted an owl.

"Never trust a Spriggin!" spat another.

The Spriggins hurled back a volley of barbed words, and the remaining few on the ground took to the air to join their brethren and engage their new enemies -- the owls. No one knew how it started, but the fighting was no longer limited to insults. Owl and Spriggin alike traded blows so terrible that several of them were sent crashing into the ground. Others smashed into the mushroom seats, making them explode in a hail of spongy projectiles. The battered and the broken soon littered the ground, their cries of pain lost to the bedlam.

At the center of it all stood Cornish Nettle. Calm and collected, he watched with dominion over the riot unfolding in front of him. Unlike Otus and Asio, who had taken off after their son, and Glenna and Dartmoor, who had cowered together to avoid the seething swarm of Spriggins and owls, Cornish was unmoved. Even his normally unflappable courtiers abandoned their posts. Arms crossed, he seemed to drink in the horror, an ominous glint in his eye adding to his unnerving repose.

"Cornish, do something!" shrieked Glenna.

"Father, make it stop!" Dartmoor pleaded, shielding himself with his hat. "You never said this would happen!"

Cornish turned his head, and peering over his shoulder at his huddled family, he gave them a smile that would turn an ogre's blood to ice. He uncrossed his arms and spread them out in front of him. He turned to face the combatants and bellowed, "FRIENDS!" This word cut through the mayhem and froze everyone in place. Even if they wanted to, the owls and Spriggins realized they couldn't really move, somehow fettered by invisible restraints, even the combatants in mid-air. All any of them could do was turn their attention to Cornish, who waited for the last of the assembly to cease their struggling and face him. Now fully bound to his gaze, the owls and Spriggins felt a strange and prevailing calm envelop them as Cornish waved his hand in an arc across the amphitheater. The phantom shackles relinquished their hold on them all, and those who had been airborne slowly floated back down to the ground. When the last had settled, he addressed them.

"Let us collect ourselves for a moment. We have witnessed a crime so horrid, it threatens to destroy the bonds of kinship binding us all. To allow this to happen would be the true tragedy, and I assure you, I will do everything within my power to prevent our world from befalling such a fate. Therefore, as current steward of Willow Hills, I decree I shall personally carry the burden of the Owl King, as well as my own, and become Monarch of All of Anglia Forest. Believe me when I say it is my most fervent desire to see the crown restored to the owls, and I do not don this mantle lightly. I alone am uniquely qualified to minister, and you, my friends, know this to be true. I should hope this solution meets with your approval, but since I shan't claim to know your hearts better than you do, I shall ask for the sake of propriety: Are there any who would oppose me in this?"

"I do!" The crowd looked up to see Otus and Asio slicing through the night sky. They dove toward the platform and perched, Otus meeting eye-to-eye with a startled Cornish. "I oppose you, Cornish Nettle. You have no such right to the crown!"

Cornish bared his teeth: "Nor do you any longer, Otus. Your reign has ended."

"On whose authority do you claim these powers? They are my son's!" Otus drew his talons.

"And where is he? You do not return with him."

"We lost track of him." The pain in Otus's voice was palpable. "We came back to find more owls to join the search party. Instead, we find you attempting to steal our son's throne. I will never let that happen!"

"So you say. Yet, the Owl King has fallen, and the crown is lost. Even if it were not, you could not reclaim it, for once it has been passed on, only its rightful owner may wield supreme authority over Anglia Forest. Sadly, your son is gone, and none feel his loss more than I, but we need to restore order before tempers flare again."

"I will not allow it," Otus bristled, puffing up his feathers and moving in on Cornish. "I will never allow it!"

"Well, it seems we are at an impasse. Ah, I know what can solve this," Cornish gestured to the crowd, "why don't we ask them whom they would have act in the King's stead? It has been done before in times of crisis. Let your former subjects decide." Cornish stepped forward on the platform and addressed the crowd. "What say you? Will you have me as your king?"

At first, nothing. The owls and Spriggins looked anxiously at each other. Then, from somewhere in the amphitheater, a few murmurs of *yes* began. More followed, building in intensity until they reached a crescendo of voices, a deafening chant proclaiming their support: *Cornish, Cornish, Cornish. . .*

Asio touched her husband's wing. "Otus, what does this mean? How can this be happening?"

"I don't know, Asio. But we must abide by this decision. It has been this way since the first trees took root in Anglia. All that is left to us is to find our son now. Without him, I don't know what will happen to any of us."

Cornish raised his hand and clenched his fist; at that moment, the chanting stopped. "My *subjects*," he drank in the word, "you have spoken, and I will humbly heed your call. Now, as your king, I know that you demand justice, so our primary concern will be to bring Annwyn Bluebell to account."

"What do you mean, Cornish Nettle?" Gwilyn stepped out from

the crowd. She had been tending to Llangollen, who had suffered a serious blow during the skirmish and been lying on the ground. "What do you mean, 'bring her to account'?"

"She has committed a very serious crime, and she must be punished."

Gwilyn gasped. "My daughter committed no crime!"

"She is a murderer."

The whole Fairy Circle seemed to shake with the uproar this charge brought, and Llangollen could bear no more. His eyes welled up, and his face reddened. Though he felt great pain, he clasped his wife's wrist and pulled himself up. It took him a moment to get to his feet, but when he did, he mustered all his strength, and his voice cut through the din: "If you dare call my daughter murderer, then I call you pretender to the throne! You are no king!"

The ruckus immediately stopped, and all eyes fell upon the battered visage of Llangollen clinging to his wife's arm for support.

Dartmoor rushed to his father's side. "Watch your tongue, old man! You address the King of Anglia Forest!"

"Mind your own, whelp!" he shot back. "I'll not sit by and allow your ilk to spread your lies! My daughter has murdered no one. It was you and that filth Blackthorn who accused Annwyn, and now this false king dares to—*HURK!*" Llangollen suddenly lost his grip on Gwilyn and fell to the ground.

"LLANGOLLEN!" Gwilyn dropped to her knees to help her husband, who was moaning and clutching the back of his neck. "Llangollen, what's wrong?" But he could not answer.

"It would seem he has succumbed to his injuries," Cornish sneered. "A casualty of the pandemonium this night has wrought, and yet another reminder of the need for order."

"I know you have done this, Cornish Nettle!" Gwilyn bawled. "You and that spawn of yours!" She focused on Dartmoor, who had curiously stepped back on the platform and appeared deep in concentration. "I will see the both of you imprisoned for this!" she wailed through streaming tears.

"SILENCE!" Cornish boomed, leaving everyone quivering. "I will not have such dissent under my reign." He turned an accusatory finger at Gwilyn. "You and your husband have threatened your king, and defended an enemy of Anglia, a murderer, no less! It is precisely this type of depravity that will rive our great society should we let it. I have no such intentions of that happening. Gwilyn Bluebell, you and your husband are no longer free to roam this wood."

"You can't stop me!" Gwilyn shot back.

"Perhaps not, woman. But I do not need to." Cornish snapped his fingers.

The shadows on the edges of the Fairy Circle came to life and slinked forth in thousands of spindly limbs. A quivering, hissing, hairy mass broke apart to reveal an army of spiders descending upon the unwitting inhabitants of the ring. The Spriggins and owls let out cries of terror at this horrid sight. And they had every reason to, for these were the Spiders of the Wolf Clan, large and powerful, but still possessed of lightning quickness. They used their superior size to force everyone to the center of the circle, while behind them, a shower of tiny orb spiders spun down from the trees and sealed off the perimeter with silk, their legs and torsos undulating. They had already sealed the canopy. The wolf spiders closed in on the center until they formed a perimeter of twitching fangs and black, lifeless eyes.

Otus burst forth. "What is the meaning of this? Why are the spiders here?"

"Yes, I know, our old nemeses the spiders. Well, they need be adversaries no longer, for I have forged an alliance with their mistress, Queen Erebus. They, whom we once called foe, we shall now call friend. Unless you have any objections, Otus." Cornish snapped his fingers again.

With frightening speed, the largest and most terrifying of the wolf spiders scrambled up the mossy base of the platform and pounced on top of it. Even the bravest among them quivered in fear, for this was no creature of the forest; this was death incarnate, a phantasm of doom that existed for the sole purpose of sowing chaos and discord in the world and snuffing out the promise of life. The onerous aura this hulk effused served the beast well; it absorbed all that was good and pure in the world and perverted it, desecrated it, for no other reason than to give him the pleasure of watching it wither, spoil and die. He was the bringer of disease. He was the defiler of souls. He was the destroyer of hope. He was the bane of the living. He was Lycurgus. And now he drew within inches of Otus's face, his smaller, lower eyes darting back and forth while his large upper eyes zeroed in on the former king. He parted his palps and let out a shrill hiss through giant black fangs. Dartmoor snickered.

"Well, Lycurgus here tells me you have had a change of heart. I'm delighted to hear it," Cornish crowed.

"Mark my words well, Nettle. I will stop you from spreading your poison," Otus scowled defiantly, even in the face of the dreaded spider.

"You may try. Now," he raised his haughty voice, "we have pressing matters at hand. Where are the Bluebells? Bring them before me."

The owls and Spriggins stepped aside, allowing two menacing wolf spiders to herd Llangollen and Gwilyn into a clearing at the base of the dais. Llangollen had recovered somewhat, but he still needed his wife's support to stay upright, for the wolf spiders' rough treatment had sapped the remnants of his already diminished strength. He raised his head and said groggily, "What's going on?"

"Just hold on to me, love," Gwilyn whispered into his ear.

"Gwilyn Bluebell, you and Llangollen stand accused of some very serious crimes. Have you anything to say on your own behalf? We shall now hear your pleas for mercy, should there be any."

"You'll hear no such thing from us, you fiend!"

"I would expect no less from a Bluebell. I fear that you leave me no choice but to detain you until I can determine a punishment befitting your sins. I will not have sympathizers of a fugitive murderer attempting to undermine our new order. Lycurgus, arrest them."

Lycurgus emitted a piercing cry. In an instant, the orb spiders flooded the amphitheater, making a disturbing rustling sound as they crawled toward the Bluebells. Gwilyn managed a horrified "No!" while hundreds of the diminutive spiders enveloped her and Llangollen, encasing them completely in silk, save for a slit for breathing. Before they could even fall to the ground, two wolf spiders grabbed them with their palps and used their fangs to hook into their sticky restraints. The crowd parted, and the spiders made their way to the edge of the Fairy Circle, where the orbs had created an opening in the webbing to let the soldiers pass with their prisoners. A shudder passed through the crowd when the spiders left the arena, and the orbs closed the breach.

"Now you see the price of disloyalty, my friends. Let us not have any more such discord. To that end, I declare that from this moment hence, all Spriggins will be confined to their homes until we can bring the wretched Annwyn Bluebell to face swift retribution for her terrible act."

"You can't do that, Nettle," Otus challenged. "We need the Spriggins to help us look for Oscar. We can only search so many places."

"I will handle that matter personally. You need not concern yourself," Cornish curled his lip.

"How dare you! You can't contain the owls in the forest, and you can't contain me. Nothing short of death will keep me from finding my son!"

Otus advanced on Cornish, his talons poised to strike, but Lycurgus jumped in front of his new master and sank a fang into Otus's neck with a sickening squish. The large owl collapsed and started convulsing.

"Otus! Otus!" Asio cradled her husband in her wings. "What have you done to him? You will rot for this, you scum!" she choked through her tears.

The outraged owls hooted, and several of them attempted to take off to attack, but the wolf spiders anticipated this and intercepted them, plucking them from the air and pinning them to the ground. The spiders made ready to dispatch their captives.

"Do you wish for more owl blood to be spilled, Asio? Call them off or they will die," Cornish warned her.

"Stand down, owls. Stand down." They complied with their queen's wish, though they burned with a desire for revenge, and they slackened their muscles and went limp; the spiders loosed their grip on the owls and let them go. Asio turned her attention from Otus to their tormentor: "In the name of my husband and son, I will see you pay for this, Cornish Nettle. Your life is now forfeit."

"Indeed. It is clear to me there are some among the owls who wish to endanger us as well. Though it pains me do to so, this disconcerting display from your former king has forced my hand. The owls will remain within the confines of the Fairy Circle until the danger has passed. Are there any more objections?"

The owls and Spriggins were visibly shaken by all they had just witnessed, and a creeping feeling of doom entered into their once joyous lives, so none dared to speak out for fear of meeting a similar fate. The wolf spiders' ambient hissing and clicking of their fangs served as a dire reminder of their position: Hundreds of thousands of glassy obsidian eyes kept watch over them, just waiting for a chance to slake their thirst on a rogue Spriggin or owl.

"Remember, this is for the good of us all," Cornish assured them. He turned to his general: "Have your warriors escort the Spriggins to their homes."

Lycurgus reared up and the Wolf Clan sprung to life. They picked the Spriggins from the owls and lined them up in rows, the smaller spiders herding while the larger ones stalked the aisles. The orbs shimmied down the web wall to incise exits for the Sprigs and their captors. The slow, sad march began out of the Fairy Circle and into the village, the wolf spiders stalking and hissing at the dejected fairies. The owls watched with despair as the last Spriggin passed through the gate, and the orbs sealed it closed. Several large spiders patrolled the circle, leaving the owls to huddle together in the center.

Glenna slithered to her husband's side and slipped her arm through his. "Well done, my dear."

Cornish smiled. "If only my work were done. Lycurgus, take your prey and his wife down to their kind. Make sure he doesn't die yet, will you?"

The giant spider gestured with his forelimbs and within seconds, there were four orbs on the platform weaving a hammock around Otus. When they finished, Lycurgus grabbed both ends in his fangs and flipped Otus onto his abdomen, where the orbs secured the wounded owl. He set his eyes on Asio.

"I suggest you go peaceably," Cornish mused.

Asio had no strength for a fight, so she obeyed, knowing she must be strong for her husband and son now. She held her head high, looked back at the Nettles, glided down, and alighted on top of a mushroom in the orchestra pit. The rest of the owls gravitated toward her. Lycurgus followed and dumped the mummified Otus next to his wife. Asio immediately went to work cutting Otus free. The other owls clenched their beaks and fought back tears while plucking their downy feathers to make a bed on the remains of the silk for their former king. They laid him in it and began their vigil.

Back on the platform, Cornish removed his arm from his wife's and turned to his son. Dartmoor bowed his head under his father's gaze. "You know what I expect of you, Dartmoor. Find the crown and bring it to me immediately. Annwyn couldn't have gotten far. And if she refuses to surrender it, let Lycurgus here persuade her to rethink her position. Let nothing stand in your way; without that crown, we might as well leave the Moonstone where it is."

"Yes father, I swear it will be done."

"Good. Lycurgus will lead you. Take your loutish pet Blackthorn with you if you must. I expect your triumphant return within a fortnight." Dartmoor turned to go, but Cornish gripped him by his elbow and pulled him close, "Do not fail me, boy. If you do not return with the stone, do not return. It will not pain me to secure another heir elsewhere."

"Yes father, I will see it done," Dartmoor winced, and Cornish released his grasp. The orbs went to work weaving a line for Dartmoor to lower himself down. Doing everything to avoid his father's stare, Dartmoor scuttled down the orb's rope and hurried off to prepare.

Glenna caressed the length of Cornish's face with a sharp fingernail, pulled him close and purred in his ear, "You have done well, my love."

CHAPTER 5

The Great Escape

Dandelion Buttercup paced her room. In general, it was not wise to sequester someone of her exceptionally energetic disposition, but in a time of crisis, it could be downright dangerous. She stomped her foot. "I gotta get out of here!" Overhead, she heard the scuttling of the spider on the roof, reacting to the vibrations. Each house had received one such unwelcome guardian. She plopped down onto her bed and rested her head on her fist. "Gotta do something . . ."

She looked around. Jeez, I am a slob, she thought, scanning the piles of wrinkled clothes and unkempt spaces which had made her pacing that much more difficult. Nothing of use. Even if I could get past the roof sentry, I'd still have to deal with all the patrols.

"Man, this stinks!" At that, she kicked a pile of canvasses, covered with clothes, when she heard a familiar *ting*. She lunged forward, and in an explosion of garments, she uncovered her tambourine and held it high. "Yes! Ha-ha, score one for the Spriggins!"

She didn't have time to ponder how she managed to misplace her tambourine in just under an hour. She had a plan.

Dandelion peeked into the hallway. The coast was clear. Of course, her parents and younger brother were downstairs; Dandelion's fidgeting and constant calls to action had caused her to be banished to her room almost immediately upon arriving home. She crept down the hall and tiptoed down the stairs, taking great pains to keep her tambourine steady. She had it wrapped in a particularly fuzzy blanket to keep the metal jingles from giving her away. A thick bathrobe provided the perfect cover for the bulky contraband and completed the ruse. If she could avoid detection, this just might work.

She peered into the kitchen from the landing. Perry and her father were at the table playing chess, while her mother prepared a late dinner. The doorway to the basement was just a few feet away from her. Unfortunately, it was also only a few feet from her family, since it was smack-dab in the middle of the hallway leading from the living room to the kitchen. She would have to be quiet, not something she was known for.

With all the stealth she could manage, she flattened herself against the baluster and inched toward the basement door. Her hand crept to the latch and clicked it loose. Luckily, no one noticed. She pulled the door open, just enough for her to squeeze through. She was almost there! And she would have made it, too, were it not for a notoriously creaky hinge, which might have well as been a hundred thousand trumpets blaring at full-volume.

"Hey, Dandelion's not in her room!" Perry pointed a condemning finger.

Poppy Buttercup looked over his shoulder to see his daughter attempting to hide behind the door, which was moving in time with her breathing. He suppressed a smile, "Oh Dandelion, why don't you come on out and tell us a story?"

Her mother, Verbena, advanced to the doorway of the kitchen. "I can only guess what you're up to this time, Dandelion Meadowfield Buttercup." The use of the middle name was never a good sign.

Dandelion slinked out from behind the door and put on her most innocent face. "I needed to get out of my room. That spider on the roof is driving me crazy! You can't expect me to stay up there listening to that. You know how I am. So, I thought maybe I could get some peace and quiet in the basement," she pleaded.

She saw Perry smile at her predicament, and she returned it with the stink-eye.

"That's a first. Dandelion wants peace and quiet," Verbena said to her husband.

Poppy looked amused. "I guess there's a first for everything. Well, my dear, considering our circumstances, perhaps the basement is the perfect solution."

"Thanks, Daddy," Dandelion smiled.

"That's not fair! She should get in trouble!" Perry squealed.

"Periwinkle Buttercup, maybe you would care for some time alone, upstairs with the spiders?" Poppy raised an eyebrow, and Perry piped down. He turned back to his daughter: "Well, go on sweetheart, find your peace and quiet down there."

"Okay, I promise not to make a sound," she said.

"That would be another first," Poppy chuckled. Dandelion made for the door. "Dandelion," he stopped her, "why are you in your bathrobe? Ah, come to think of it, don't tell me."

Dandelion blew him a kiss and disappeared into the basement.

"I just don't know what gets into her sometimes." Verbena shook her head and got back to preparing supper. Poppy faced Perry, and the game was on.

Now that she was alone, Dandelion quickly lost the robe and unwrapped her tambourine. She attempted a tentative tap on it to see if it stirred any movement upstairs. Nothing. She knelt down on the dirt floor and placed her tambourine flush with the ground. She rapped on its rim to produce a series of faint tings. She waited a bit before putting an ear to the ground. It wasn't long before she heard what she was waiting for. From somewhere below her in the soil, a squishy sound grew louder and louder. The noise tickled her ear as it got closer, so she sat up, wearing an expectant grin. It wasn't long before two worms poked their heads out through the floor.

"You rang?" Wiggles asked his friend as he twisted about, trying to untangle himself from his partner Twitch. Dandelion watched the two worms wriggle and jiggle until they were finally separated.

"I need you guys to do me a favor."

"What is it?"

"Get all your friends together and dig a tunnel out of the village. I need to get out of here and get help to fight the spiders."

Twitch shot up to attention. "What spiders?"

"Look, I don't have time to go into it right now, but we're all in big trouble. Annwyn and Oscar are missing, Cornish has taken over, and the village is crawling with spiders!"

"Whoa, I think I'll just lay low for a while," Wiggles whistled.

"So, can you guys dig me a tunnel? I need to get out of here."

"Just one? No problem," Wiggles replied. "I could do that with my eyes closed, if I had eyes."

"Well, about that, I actually need you to dig three tunnels. One for me, one for Pooka and one for Ash. I need their help, and we need to get past all the spiders unnoticed if we want to escape."

"Is that all? I thought you were going to put us to work," Wiggles joked. Twitch sighed disapprovingly at his overly optimistic partner.

"Thanks, you guys, you're the best."

Wiggles saluted. "Toil in the soil, that's our motto. Just wait here. We'll send word when we're finished. In the meantime, if I were you, I'd figure out a way to hide the fact that you're about to have gaping hole in your basement floor. We can patch it up later, but your folks'll have a couple questions if they see it."

"Already covered," she winked.

"Alright, just be ready." Wiggles and Twitch put it in reverse and squiggled back into the earth.

Now, Dandelion needed to get word to her friends, but this would require a trip upstairs. For a veteran of many capers, this would be a cinch. She re-wrapped her tambourine, put her robe back on, and dashed up the stairs. She then zipped up to the second floor with Poppy calling after her, "Everything alright, sweetheart?"

"Yep," she blurted.

Dandelion rushed into her room, tripping over wayward clutter and landing on the floor with an indignant *oof!* The spider twittered on the roof. She picked herself up and set about her next task, summoning Flicker. Hmmm, gotta distract that spider somehow, she thought, once again scanning her room. A-ha! Behind her easel, she spotted a broom, one of her mother's constant reminders to clean up. Dandelion never thought she'd see the day when she was glad to see one of those. She took off her robe, unwrapped her tambourine, and placed it near the window.

Then she grabbed the broom and once again peered into the hallway. Everyone was still downstairs. Good. She made a beeline for her parents' room at the end of the hall. Once inside, she jumped on their bed and steadied herself. Gripping the broom right above the bristles, she held it upright and pounded on the ceiling with the tip of the handle. Almost instantly she heard the sentry pattering overhead.

This was it!

Dandelion dropped the broom and bolted down the hallway back into her room. She flew straight for the window and cracked it open. She clutched her tambourine and patted a muted pattern: *ta-ting-ting-ting*. She repeated it a few more times, and then backed away from the window. The spider had returned from his investigation. Dandelion sat as patiently as she could. She was back to pacing when she heard something.

"Psst, hey, Dandy."

In crawled Flicker, the most intrepid lightning bug in Anglia. He flew over to Dandelion and landed on her waiting hand. "You must have something important to tell me, making me dodge all those beasts out there. Night flying's a lot less fun when you gotta turn your tail light off." He sympathetically lit his bottom. "So, what's up?"

"I need you to get a message to my friends. I need you to tell

Pooka and Ash to meet me in the tunnel the worms are digging under their houses. Tell them we're going to escape and get help. And tell them they need to bring their instruments. Okay?"

"Whoo, that's a tall order. I'll do what I can. It won't be easy though; those spiders are tough to duck. We barely escaped the Fairy Circle the first time, and a lot of us bugs weren't so lucky."

"I know, Flicks. Please be careful out there."

"Not to worry, Dandy. I'll be fine. I got over here, didn't I? Uh, speaking of which, how am I supposed to get back out? I barely got past that furry nightmare on the way in, and he's right above us now."

"Don't worry, just wait 'til you hear a bunch of thumping. That'll distract the spider long enough for you to get out."

"Sounds like a plan," Flicker affirmed with a glowing backside.

"Great, meet me back here when you're done, and we'll go into the tunnel together," Dandelion snuck in.

"What's this about me going in the tunnel?" he said, raising a quizzical antenna.

"C'mon Flicks, you don't want to miss out on an adventure like this, do you? Besides, I can't see in the dark, and you can light up all you want underground with no spiders lurking around."

To a lightning bug who had to douse his lamp to avoid becoming a spider-snack, this was an enticing offer. "I'll probably regret this, but, you got it, Dandy."

"Alright, wait for my signal then. And good luck, Flicks." Dandelion rushed back into her parents' room and resumed banging the broom handle on the ceiling. Wanting to make sure that her friend had plenty of time to escape, she misjudged how long it would take for her mother to find out what she was doing.

"Dandelion Meadowfield Buttercup, what on earth are you doing?" Verbena was in the doorway, and she was not pleased.

"I was, uh, cleaning off your bed." Dandelion began sweeping their comforter.

"Well, that's enough cleaning for one night, young lady. Your supper's ready, so go wash up and take your place at the table directly," Verbena scolded.

"Yes, Mom." Dandelion scooted past her mother and went to get ready for dinner.

Verbena shook her head. "Sometimes I wonder about that girl."

After supper, the Buttercup family went their separate ways and engaged in the activities that normally brought them comfort in better times: Poppy dozed on the sofa; Verbena drew herself a hot bath; and Perry tried playing with some toys in his room. Dandelion had also retired to her bedroom, but not to relax. She excavated her room, recovered her knapsack, and proceeded to fill it with supplies: a blanket, a pillow, some warm clothes, smuggled food, medicine, her tambourine. She then spent a good half-hour crafting the perfect body double for her bed. Now, she had to wait for Flicker to return, but she was worried. She left the window open slightly, and she hoped her savvy friend would be able to elude the spider without the benefit of her broomstick theatrics. These thoughts fueled her boundless anxiety, so she continued work on a painting, her favorite hobby and quite possibly the only thing in the world that could keep her from causing a commotion in her current circumstances.

Dandelion jumped a foot into the air and nearly smeared her most recent masterpiece when she heard a voice loudly whisper "Dandy!" in her ear.

She whipped around and there, floating in mid-air with a grin on his face, was Flicker. "Jeez, next time give me a heads-up, Flicks. You scared me half to death."

"Sorry, Dandy. Who knew you were so jumpy? Oh that's right, everybody," he sniggled.

"Ha-ha," she deadpanned. "Are you ready to go?"

His posterior lit up.

"Okay, let's go."

Dandelion put on her cloak and knapsack. Flicker buzzed over and hid himself in the folds of her cloak's hood. She made sure the lightning bug had doused his lamp before checking the hall and creeping down the stairs. Her father's snoring assured her that this trip to the basement would go more smoothly than the last. She sidled to the door, opened it just enough to avoid its creaking, slipped through, and clicked it closed behind her. Once down the stairs, she rushed over to a small mound of dirt on the ground. She suffered her second major fright of the night when she knelt down and fell headfirst through the dirt floor, only her legs sticking out of the sinkhole. She found herself face-to-tip with Wiggles.

"Careful Dandelion, the ground's not stable up there," he smirked.

"Thanks for the tip," she spit out a mouthful of dirt. "Are the tunnels complete?"

"Everything's finished. How 'bout a challenge next time?" Wiggles razzed her.

"Sure thing. I could do without the trap door, though." Dandelion pulled herself completely into the tunnel. It was wide enough for her to turn around, get a brown towel from her pack, and plug the opening. She was pleased her plan was going along flawlessly, minus the face-plant, and they would be able to escape the village unnoticed. "Where are Pooka and Ash?"

"They're already down here, just up ahead. Allow me." Wiggles shimmied to the front of the tunnel while Twitch brought up the rear. "Everyone ready?"

"I just have to turn on my light," Dandelion checked her hood to make sure Flicker was still there, considering him a safeguard against another dirty tumbling act. "Flicks, you in there?"

Flicker popped out onto her head and lit up on cue. "Bright enough for ya?" he beamed. Flicker took pride in his vividness.

"You light up my life, Flicks," Dandelion snickered at her headlamp. The four started down the tunnel, Wiggles in the lead, Flicker riding the crawling Dandelion, and Twitch bringing up the rear. "The ground's awfully mushy," Dandelion said, each movement producing a sloppy, sloshing sound. Feeling really slimy, she paused to look at her hands. "What is all this? How did you manage to get it all muddy down here?"

"Hazard of the trade, I'm afraid," Wiggles giggled.

"What do you mean?"

"Sorry, I guess I soiled myself."

She felt the words building in her belly, and before she could stop herself, she screamed, "Worm poop—GROSS!!!" Dandelion wallowed in the muck and winced; she could feel the digested soil squishing between her fingers like jelly. "*Bleck!*"

"Hey! That's Mother Nature's finest! You won't find a better fertilizer anywhere." Twitch and Wiggles didn't really take offense, for they were proud of their handiwork.

"Best not to ask questions you don't care to hear the answers to," Twitch said dryly. He nudged Dandelion to keep her from lollygagging.

They kept moving, and a ways down the tunnel, Dandelion began to hear the faint sound of voices she knew. They were close to Pooka and Ash. "Let's hurry Wiggles, I can hear the boys." Wiggles quickened from a snail's pace to a worm's pace, but it still wasn't fast enough to suit Dandelion. "Ooh, you guys are too slow." Dandelion pumped her limbs as fast as she could in the tunnel, and Wiggles barely had enough time to burrow out of her way. She followed the voices of her friends, so she lowered her head, plied even more speed, rounded a corner and *THUNK,* smacked heads with an already cranky and crawling Ash. The unsuspecting Spriggin took the full force of the battering ram, known as the top of Dandelion's head, directly in the center of his forehead. Pain crackled in his skull, and stars flashed before his eyes; he dropped to his elbows, immediately cupping the contusion.

"OWW! Why don't you watch where you're going?" Ash squawked. He and Dandelion both rubbed their noggins.

"Hey, if you hadn't noticed, it's kind of dark down here, okay?"

"Yeah? That's why you have these." Ash motioned behind himself with a hitchhiker's thumb. Two of Flicker's brothers, Sparky and Flash, produced themselves from within the confines of Pooka's poncho. Flicker, who had performed a last-minute maneuver to escape death-by-head butt, flew over to them. The three lightning bugs blinked their bottoms at each other in greeting.

"Thanks, I'll remember that the next time we have to tunnel out of the village," Dandelion rolled her eyes. "Hey Pooka, you back there?" She peered past Ash to see her friend behind him in the tunnel.

"I'm here. Hi, Dandy." He gave a little wave.

The Flicker Brothers flew over to Ash to inspect the damage. The moaning Spriggin grimaced his way onto his back, and the hovering lightning bugs simultaneously lowered their lamps to reveal a throbbing, purple lump forming on Ash's head. Flicker flashed repeatedly, a sign of laughter. "Well, Ash, the good news is we found the only Sprig with a head harder than yours."

"Ha, ha." Ash tested the tender knot with a finger. "Ow! That's just dandy, Dandy. By the way, what took you so long? Off fooling around again?"

"No, Ash, I was organizing our plan to find help. You know, you should thank me! Maybe I finally knocked some sense into you!" She punched him in the arm, not needing to be reminded about her reputation for goofing off right now.

"So, what's your big plan?" Ash asked with his usual skepticism.

Well, Wiggles, Twitch and the other worms have built tunnels to the edge of Willow Hills. We'll creep past all the spiders up there, come up right at the entrance to the forest, and make our escape," Dandelion announced triumphantly.

Pooka stuck his head out again. "Then what?" He and Ash looked at her expectantly.

"Oh, uh, I guess I didn't plan that far ahead. Any ideas?"

Pooka spoke with a resolve not often heard in his voice: "We must find Annwyn. If we find her and Oscar and bring them back, we'll have a chance to defeat Cornish and the spiders."

"But we don't even know if they're still alive. Otus and Asio couldn't find them, and they're owls. What if the spiders got them?"

"I know Annwyn is still alive, I can just feel it. No matter what you decide to do, I'm going to find her."

His words hung heavily in the air for a moment before Ash broke the tension: "Count me in."

"Okay, let's do it. So, you guys ready? I hope you brought everything," Dandelion said. "Did you bring your instruments?" She knew Flicker gave them the explicit instructions on what to bring, but it never hurt to double-check.

"About that," Pooka began, "my drum is still at the Fairy Circle. I had to abandon it once we were surrounded."

Dandelion's face turned pale.

"Maybe he won't need it," Ash ventured hopefully.

"No! We need that drum, Ash! You know that. Without it, we might as well go back home and hope this all works itself out," Dandelion insisted. "Our music is our magic. Think about all the great stories about Spriggins going on quests and defeating monsters and demons. What do they all have in common? At some point, the heroes used music to solve a problem or slay a beast. Don't you pay attention to anything, you dunderhead?"

"But I have my mandolin, and you've got your tambourine, so that's gotta count for something," Ash countered.

"Have you ever heard Pooka drum? When he hits that thing, even the mountains shake! Our instruments can't do that! We've never been that far out of Willow Hills before. I don't know what's out there, do you? If we've got that drum, we've got a chance. Without it, we won't even get past those orbs, who'll just string us up and leave us to hang, or worse!"

Ash knew she was right, and besides, once Dandelion made up her mind, no force on earth could change it. "Okay, Dandy." He shuddered, knowing what they would be facing going back into the Fairy Circle.

"We can do this. No group of cruddy spiders can stop us!" She smiled, and it reassured Ash. Then she turned her attention to Twitch and Wiggles. "Hey guys, would you mind doing me one more favor?"

"Sure thing," Wiggles said.

"We need a tunnel to the Fairy Circle."

"And the hits just keep on comin'. You guys'll have to wait here while we round up our buddies and get started, so just sit tight. We'll be back." Wiggles began burrowing, and Twitch waggled behind.

The three friends found themselves with some extra time on their hands, so it was a bit of good luck when Dandelion sat down and discovered jacks in her pack. They threw a few spirited but sloppy matches with the Flicker Brothers' assistance. Before one round had a chance to erupt into an argument over a sudden rule change, Wiggles bored through the wall opposite the potentially ugly scene. "Hey, what's going on here? Oh, were you losing again, Dandy? I should've known."

"I wasn't losing! Ash is a cheater!"

"Me?! If I had a coin for every time you—"

"Uh, guys, I think we have more important things to worry about," Pooka inserted.

"Yeah, everyone knows you can't play with Dandy," Wiggles said. Dandelion made to protest this scandalous accusation, but Wiggles wisely curtailed her remonstrations: "So, come in, your tunnel's ready."

"It's ready? And how're we supposed to get in there, huh?" Ash grumbled, skeptically inspecting the wall of dirt from which the worm extended himself. "You gotta dig a hole we can actually fit into.

I don't know if you noticed, but some of us are just a little too big to squeeze into a wormhole, and my head's taken enough of a beating already."

Twitch popped out next to his companion in the wall. "Not to worry. You only need crawl straight ahead, good sir. Just do give us a moment to make ourselves scarce."

"See ya on the other side!" Wiggles and his brother slurped back into the dirt wall.

"Buncha wise guys," Ash stewed. He crawled forward to the wall and examined up-close the tiny holes left by the worms. "I don't see how we're supposed to get in there."

"There's only one way to find out!" Armed with the knowledge gained from her basement tumbling act, Dandelion took this opportunity to kick her friend right in his butt, sending him face-first through the wall. The thin layer of dirt the worms had left on strands of mucus parted like beads, and even though Ash was unharmed, he was not very happy.

"If only we had time to fight about this," Ash fumed. "C'mon!" He grabbed Dandelion by her arm and yanked her into the tunnel. Pooka followed behind, chuckling while Flicker, Flash and Sparky lit their hindquarters and landed on top of their assigned Spriggins' heads. Wiggles and Twitch popped back out of the wall next to Dandelion's face.

"Here you go, one deluxe tunnel to go. Just follow it all the way to the Fairy Circle. You'll come out underneath a nice big umbrella mushroom in the orchestra pit. All the owls are up there too, so we passed word about what's going down, and they're waiting for you. And don't worry, once you're through, we'll backfill these tunnels so the spiders won't find 'em. Good luck guys, I wish I could come with you, but I'm the leader of the underground movement." Wiggles stretched out and planted a sticky kiss on Dandelion's cheek. "Be careful."

"We will be. And don't worry, we'll be back with help before you know it." She smiled at the worms, and they were off.

The Spriggins and their insect-headlamps advanced down the tunnel, and since this one was a bit larger than the last, they were able to crouch and move much more quickly. After a while, the passageway started sloping upward and became narrower, so they had to revert to crawling. Dandelion, who had taken the lead, came to the exit underneath the floor of the Fairy Circle. It was just like the way in: The worms had secreted strands of mucus across the opening and covered them with dirt, making for a pliable and camouflaged egress. Dandelion cautiously reached out and parted the filaments. To her delight, they weren't as sticky as the other strands thanks to the special dirt of the Fairy Circle. She poked the top of her head out and saw several owl feet and bodies surrounding the perimeter of a mushroom.

"Hey," she whispered. "It's me, Dandelion. We're here."

One of the owls mechanically turned his head; it was Oden, a particularly handsome and crafty owl who served in the capacity of warrior and bodyguard to the King. He whispered back, "We've been waiting for you, but put those lights out, we can see them out here!"

"Flicks, turn off!" The lightning bug brothers complied, and Dandelion turned her attention back to Oden: "So what's the plan?"

"The worms filled us in, so we found Pooka's drum and have it hidden under here. And we've got this mushroom surrounded, so you can get out unnoticed, but there are spiders all over the place. Ludwig here's going to cause a distraction while I, Oakley and Sadé sneak you over to the web wall. We'll cut a hole in it, and you guys'll make your exit."

"Sounds good. Hey, could you kick that over to me?" Dandelion motioned to the drum. "It's probably a good idea to get this thing hidden before we come out." Oakley nonchalantly nudged the noisy instrument to her, and she snatched it up and disappeared back down the hole.

"Pooka, here's your drum." She handed it to him, and he stuffed it into his pack.

"So what's the deal?" Ash queried. Dandelion gave the boys the low-down.

"What about us? We want to help," Flicker said, and his brothers lit up for a moment.

"You guys hide yourselves on us, and we'll smuggle you out. It might be a good idea to have some light out there in the forest. Just keep it dim until we're out of here," Dandelion said.

"No problem." The lightning bugs nestled into their Spriggins' coats.

"Ready?" Dandelion looked back at her friends.

Ash gave her a thumbs-up. The three Spriggins lifted themselves out of the hole and remained crouching. They all heard sobbing coming from over their heads.

"What's all the crying?" Dandelion asked.

"It's Otus, he's dying," Oden replied somberly. "It's the bite from that big spider. He's lying on top of this mushroom, and we're trying our best to halt the poison, but he grows worse by the minute. Asio won't let the spiders see her grief, but some of the others can't contain theirs."

The news seared the Spriggins; Dandelion bowed her head to hide her own tears, and Ash placed a comforting hand on her shoulder, which was seconded by Pooka. Their spirits reached their nadir, a depth of sorrow they never could have imagined before tonight, but they knew that this was not the time for lamentations. Dandelion put on her bravest face and steeled herself, thanks to Ash and Pooka's reassuring embrace.

"I know it's difficult, but we don't have much time. Let's get you out of here. Are you ready?" Oden asked. They shook their heads in unison. That was all Oden needed: He signaled to Ludwig, who left his post on the mushroom and launched into the air. He zipped across the amphitheater, clipped Ulric, Lycurgus's lieutenant and the main guard on top of the central platform, and lodged himself firmly in the webbing encasing the Fairy Circle. He began twisting and flailing about yelling, "I can't take it any more! I need out! LET ME OUT!!!"

Ulric motioned with his forelimbs, dispatching a crew of wolf and orb spiders to investigate this nuisance and cut him loose, leaving few eyes to watch over Oden and his escapees. While the spiders continued their task of untangling the distraught owl, Oden, Oakley, Sadé and the hunkered-down Spriggins crept toward the web wall without being noticed. Once there, Oden stood point and spread his wings to allow Oakley and Sadé the cover needed to use their talons and cut through the webbing. Luckily, Ludwig's convulsions kept the few sentries not dealing with the disturbance from noticing the vibrations this caused and within moments, the owls' razor-sharp talons sliced an opening for the Spriggins.

"Now's your chance, go!" Sadé whispered to them. The Spriggins burst through the hole and took off.

At just that moment, Ulric sensed an odd vibration and turned from the Ludwig-spectacle to notice Oden at the wall with his wings spread. He let out a sound like steam escaping a kettle, and instantly, the remaining guards descended upon the owls and pounced, pinning them to the ground. Ulric let out a nightmarish cry when he saw the gaping hole in the wall. Someone had escaped! With another hiss, he sent a contingent of orbs to the opening, which they widened. His warriors already knew what to do; they converged on the opening and sped through to chase down the fugitives.

Ulric came down from the platform and stood in front of the downed owls. One of his guards lifted Oden's head, and Ulric bared his fangs with a seething sibilance. Even though he did not speak the spider-tongue, Oden knew that they were in mortal danger.

"Do your worst, filth!" Oden spit in his face.

Ulric didn't seem to notice. He raised a back leg, and the orbs descended on the owls, wrapping them for transport to the prison. Ludwig had been cut from the wall and received the same treatment. The guards hoisted them and carried them out of the Fairy Circle. Ulric turned his onyx gaze on Asio and the others keeping watch over Otus. The remaining owls watched with somber resignation as the orbs closed the escape route.

"We need to help them, Asio," a young owl named Calliope urged.

"No, we all knew the risk involved when we agreed to help the Spriggins escape. We will remain and watch over Otus." She never once dropped her eyes from Ulric's.

Dandelion, Pooka and Ash ran as fast as they could. They knew it wouldn't be long before the guards came after them, and if they could clear the village and get into the woods, they could use their knowledge of the forest to evade the spiders. They kept to the outskirts of the village, weaving their way in and out of the shadows, trying not to draw the attention of the spiders already prowling the streets. They had to get to the westerly clearing, for the underbrush lining this part of the village was too thick and brambly, and would hamper their movement just enough to make them easy prey. They were close to their goal when Dandelion looked behind her and saw a wolf spider, a scout, following their path.

"Guys! There's a spider on our tail!" she cried through sharp exhalations.

Pooka allowed himself a quick glance. "I don't think he's seen us yet. C'mon, we're almost there!"

The three of them ran even harder. They came out to the clearing, a stretch of grass and dirt surrounded by the thorny thicket. Keeping low, they paused for a second.

"It looks like the coast is clear," Ash whispered. "That scout'll be on us soon and bring all his buddies. Let's go." Crouching, Ash took a few steps forward. He thought the ground felt funny, kind of hollow for some reason. He stopped. "Something's not right here."

"We don't have time! The scout's coming up on us and he's not alone!" Dandelion trembled.

A moth flew in front of them into the clearing, and it caught their attention. They watched in horror when the ground opened up and swallowed the moth in an instant.

"Ahh!" Dandelion shrieked. "Trapdoor spiders! We'll never get past them!"

Unfortunately, Dandelion's scream alerted the wolf spiders to where they were. Pooka looked down the trail and saw them rapidly approaching. The spiders patrolling the nearby village abandoned their posts and scurried toward the terrified Spriggins. No fewer than a hundred warriors now bore down on them.

Dandelion hid her head in her hands. "We're going to die."

"Not yet we're not," Pooka calmly stated. He pulled his drum from his pack.

"What're you gonna do with that?" Ash trembled.

"Just follow me." Pooka stood and hit his drum as hard as he could. The *WHUMP* caused the hundreds of trapdoors to pop up from the sheer force of the vibration. Without hesitation, he charged into the arachnid minefield, pounding his drum, *WHUMP-WHUMP-WHUMP*, each beat exposing the subterranean spiders' hatches. Ash pulled Dandelion to her feet, and they followed Pooka, weaving their way through the trapdoors. But their pursuers didn't have to contend with being snatched from below and hit the clearing at full speed.

"They're right behind us!" Dandelion yelped. "GO! GO!"

Flicker stuck his head out from under her cloak and saw the spiders gaining on them. "Whoa! This can't be good! Alright fellas, let's slow these beasts down!" He flew up in the air with his brothers following. Not known as the most agile insects in the forest, Flicker and his brothers nevertheless skillfully bobbed and weaved in front of the spiders, disorienting them by flashing their lights in their faces. They caused just enough commotion to slow the spiders' progress and allow the Spriggins to put some distance between them and certain death.

Strangely, Pooka's drum had begun glowing with a vermilion hue, which became stronger and stronger with each strike. His drumbeats were becoming so mighty that Dandelion and Ash could feel the ground moving. Even the tireless spiders fell behind, hobbled by the force overloading their sensors. The light provided by the drumming allowed the friends to see they were now past the clearing and nearing the open wood. Pooka stopped once past the danger of the trapdoors, and allowed his bewildered friends, including the Flicker Brothers, to pass him. He faced the wolf spiders, who were just a few yards away and closing in rapidly, and stood his ground, continually pounding his drum, which gave off an even stronger light now.

"POOKA!" Dandelion wailed.

The mass of spiders was now upon Pooka, rearing up and exposing their fangs, but he did not falter. An image of Annwyn flashed in his mind. From somewhere deep inside himself, he let out a primal yell and hit his drum harder than he ever thought possible. The drum exploded in a burst of red light and emitted a shockwave that overwhelmed the spiders and sent them flying backwards. They fell on their backs and crinkled up in a mound of twitching limbs and broken bodies, while their juices seeped into the ground.

"Let's go, Pooka!" Ash grabbed his dazed friend, and the three of them made for the safety of the deep woods.

CHAPTER 6

Woodland Council

Dressed in the earthen-colored tunic, leggings and boots provided her, Annwyn stood in the cavernous dock alongside Fein as Emmlen summoned her golden ship from the depths. The vessel silently glided to the dock and moored itself, its ropes moving of their own volition. Freed from her trance, Emmlen pulled Annwyn aside. "Now you must depart this place. Fein will guide you across the lake and leave you not too far from your destination. From there, your ring will guide you to where you need to go."

"And where is that?"

"I cannot say, for I no longer have any control over these events. Trust in the Emerald Flower. The ring obeys your will, just as you abide by its."

"*Its* will? Is this thing alive?"

"In a fashion it is, since this ring is an instrument of the life force of its wearer, drawing upon her strength to magnify its own."

"But all those things you said it could do…I don't have any powers like that."

"Do you not? Perhaps before long you will come to know differently. I understand your hesitancy, Annwyn, and I sense your mind is clouded by doubts, insecurities. You will learn to shake these bugbears free, and when you do, you will come to know a great deal more about the ring, and yourself."

Annwyn stood silently, staring down at the ring with an apprehension approaching fear and struggling to come to terms with the turn her life had taken. Memories of life in Willow Hills seemed faded and distant now, the last beams of light struggling on the horizon against a bleak dusk. The world no longer made any sense, and maybe it never would again. Thankfully, she found momentary respite at the sight of Oscar, led by Fern and Flax, emerging from a vestibule and hovering over to where they were standing. His damaged eye had healed enough from the water fairies' magic for the patch to be removed; the pupil of his left eye had become permanently dilated, and it reminded Annwyn of a solar eclipse -- a large black disk surrounded by a band of fiery yellow. Her heart sunk at the sight of his injury, but Oscar's spirits were not so easily dampened. "Am I late?" he queried, his trademark grin peeking out.

"Nope, you've got perfect timing." Annwyn hugged her friend.

Fein cleared his throat, so the two separated and turned to face Emmlen. "May the fortunes smile upon you, Annwyn of the Bluebell Clan and King Oscar, for if you do not prevail in your conquest, none will." She gently laid a kiss upon Annwyn's forehead and visited the same honor on Oscar.

Annwyn gulped a little. "Thank you for everything. We couldn't continue on without your help." She was frightened by the prospect of leaving her gracious host and the relative safety of the lake to face an uncertain future, but she would not show it.

"I owe you a debt I can never repay," Oscar said, bowing slightly. "After all this is finished, know that you will always be welcome in Anglia Forest so long as I am King."

Emmlen smiled in return.

Fein then led the comrades aboard the boat and took the captain's position at the helm. The passengers of the golden ship set sail for the sandy shore, unaware of what peril might lie ahead. Emmlen stood watching as they vanished under the glassy pool of the bay, hoping their venture would be triumphant, for so much depended on it.

Fein took Annwyn and Oscar along the same route as their descent to the great palace, the owl taking in the visions for the first time. "Graybeak's feathers! I can't believe it! This is incredible!" He rubbed his one good eye to make sure what he was seeing was indeed real: All sorts of underwater creatures swam past them in a tapestry of fins, gills, scales, shells, tentacles and tendrils that swirled, dashed and darted more elegantly than any flock of birds Oscar had ever encountered in the open sky. Their choreography mesmerized the Owl King, and he let it work its magic on his mind, filling him with the type of wonderment usually reserved for children.

Annwyn laid a gentle hand on his back.

"I saw it on the way in," she smiled at him.

The ship maneuvered to the surface of the waters and broke through; the sky was a dark metallic gray and the fog immediately enveloped them, leaving the two passengers feeling lost and adrift. Closing her eyes, Annwyn could feel the cool, damp kisses of the fog on her face as the boat silently gilded across the lake. Eventually, the mists parted somewhat, creating a path to the lakeside. The vessel pulled parallel to the shore and came to a halt.

"We have arrived," Fein announced, the first time he had spoken the entire trip. He disembarked, offered his hand to Annwyn, and she climbed down from the vessel. Oscar fluttered to land on shaky wings. "Good luck, Miss Annwyn and Oscar the King. Fare thee well."

Letting go of his hand, Annwyn bowed. "Thank you." Oscar gave a nod to the fairy.

Fein bowed his head and returned to the helm. In an instant, the boat had disappeared amongst the mists, and Oscar and Annwyn were left standing alone.

"I guess it's just you and me," Annywn said, slinging an arm around him. "Our path's gotta be around here somewhere." She chewed her lip a little bit, looked up and down the shoreline for a while, turning this way and that, but she saw nothing. The silvery sands melted into the dense forest line, and one section of it looked the same as the next in the dim light.

"So, what now?" Oscar chimed in.

"Good question…" she trailed off, scanning the shrouded horizon. Then it happened. She felt a slight tug, as if an invisible tendril had slipped around her wrist. This feeling was commensurate with an odd buzzing from somewhere inside of her, as if her whole body had begun purring. She looked down at her hand, not sure what was happening. But there it was again. She dropped her arm from her friend. "Oscar, something weird's going on."

"Like what?"

"Like this."

The Emerald Flower cast forth a mild glow from its stones. Annwyn's right arm raised itself and pulled her down the beach, the ring's sparkling growing in intensity with each step. Her body tingled and buzzed along with the ring.

"Wait up!" Oscar took to the air, fumbled a little bit before balancing, and followed Annwyn, who had taken on a frenetic pace. His diminished sight and the thick fog made it almost impossible to see her, even with the light cast by the ring, but he could still hear her thumping footfalls on the sand. Barely in control, Annwyn raced down the shore until the force on her arm slackened and fell away as the Emerald Flower's beacon faded. The energy in her body tapered off, so she came to a stop. Oscar tried his best to avoid his suddenly stationary friend, but even an owl couldn't dodge her in this fog, and he slammed into her, sending them both sprawling into the beach in a poof of feathers.

"Smooth flying, ace," Annwyn grumbled, rubbing sand from her face.

"Thanks, next time, tell me you're puttin' on the brakes." Oscar stood and shook out, showering Annwyn with a spray of sand.

"Ahhh! Oscar, watch what you're doing!"

"Sorry."

"Besides, I didn't stop, the ring did."

"What ring?" Oscar looked down at Annwyn's hand at the dormant circlet. "Wow, where'd you get that?"

"It's the Emerald Flower ring. Emmlen gave it to me. She said it was worn by the Matriarch of my clan, and I'm meant to wear it, whatever that means."

"What does it do?"

Annwyn shrugged her shoulders. "I don't really know for sure. It's supposed to guide us on our way -- that's what Emmlen said anyway -- so I guess that's what it's doing, though I could do without it yanking on my arm."

"Feisty little sucker, isn't it?"

Then, the tingling began inside of Annwyn again and light stirred inside the Emerald Flower. She held up her hand, and an aura grew from within the ring, burning with such intensity that it cleft the fog in front of them, revealing a passageway. At its end stood a dark and foreboding break in the forest; the gnarled trees on either side of the archway twisted together, their branches intertwining like decrepit fingers. They walked to the entrance and stood for a minute, gathering the courage to move forward. Even the viridian light from the ring did not pierce its black veil.

Oscar's eye expanded to a black disc as he took in the darkness oozing from the woods. "Are we supposed to go in there?"

Annwyn swallowed hard: "Well, it would be quite a coincidence if we weren't."

"I'm a firm believer in coincidence, so let's go find a little nicer spot to enter."

"Sorry, Oscar. Emmlen told me the ring would guide me, and it brought us here. This is where we need to go."

"Or maybe the ring is trying to tell you that going down this path isn't a good idea."

"I guess we'll find out."

They dared one more look back at the lake, and then they took their first step onto the path and into the eager wood.

Meanwhile, Lycurgus prowled on another wicked path, followed closely by Dartmoor and Rowan, each riding atop a wolf spider. Dartmoor's ride carried another traveler, a much smaller wolf spider, known only as the Messenger, while Rowan's carried several orb spiders in case they stumbled upon any unsuspecting prey. The dastardly group had but one immediate goal: to secure the crown and see its safe return to Cornish. Lycurgus drew to a stop, causing the others to follow suit. Focusing his rear eyes on the Spriggins, he spoke inside their heads with a harsh whisper: *Fan the wood and search every inch, the crown cannot be far. Alert me immediately if you find it or the Spriggin who stole it. I will handle all of this personally.*

The deathly cold voice rattled inside Rowan's skull, blurring his vision and inducing a swell of queasiness and dry retching. The paroxysms pitched Rowan from his saddle, and he still shook after he picked himself up off the ground. "Damnation! What's goin' on aroun' here? How'sat he's talkin' in m'head?!"

"Settle yourself. You'll grow accustomed to the effects of spiderspeak soon enough," Dartmoor reproached him. "My father has seen to it that the spiders and we understand each other now. It makes it so much easier to be friends."

"I don' like it one bit! I didn' know we'd be doin' all this! You jus' tol' me we'd be pullin' a prank on them dirty Bluebells! You didn't say nothin' 'bout no spiders, crowns or killin'! It just ain't right!"

"Rowan, don't be so infantile. You're embarrassing yourself."

"Me?! You got a lot a' gumption ta—"

Continue your bickering and we'll be returning with one less Spriggin. The giant spider's crippling voice dashed Rowan to the ground, and he curled up into a ball, quivering and whimpering. *Get back on your mount and look for that crown. If you find it, I may yet let you live.*

"I'd do what he says," Dartmoor intoned. Rowan scurried back to his ride and climbed back into the saddle. "Are we done with our little tantrums?" Rowan drooped his head and nodded. "Excellent.

Now then, Lycurgus, you head north. Rowan, go west, and I'll take to the east. Your spiders can do what you promised, can they not, Lycurgus?"

The spider gave him no reply.

The Spriggins quickly quit the glowering beast and set about prowling the wood, scouring it for any sign of the missing crown. The tiny hairs covering the spiders' bodies flickered constantly, waiting for the slightest vibration from the metal crown on the chilly night air. Dartmoor invoked an incantation, bestowing on him and Rowan the Eyes of Twilight charm, which rendered blackest night into brightest day. For hours on end they searched, making paths up and down their vectors, investigating every rustle, crackle and snap in the woods. Every so often, the spiders surprised an unfortunate forest-dweller and fell upon them, devouring them so horribly that the mortified Spriggins could barely register the blood-curdling screams of the victims.

After finishing feasting on a fawn, Lycurgus felt a small twinge amongst the hairs on his forelimbs, and this one was different from the dozens of other fluctuations and reverberations so common in a forest of this kind: This one growled with power. The spider spun around slowly, following the tugging on his legs until it intensified, alerting him to the provenance of the rippling tremors. Now he could feel where it was, whatever it was, just ahead on the road to the

Emerald Lake. Enticed by the waves of energy tickling his body, Lycurgus pulsed ahead to their source, gliding across the forest floor with a dire urgency. There it was, the Crown of the Owl King. He pounced upon the treasure and snatched it with his palps. *I have it!*

Rowan nearly fell off his mount when the orbs riding with him ran across his lap and flew to Lycurgus, descending on the spoil and wrapping it in silk. The Messenger jumped to the ground and scurried over to the orbs, which climbed on his back and fastened the crown to him.

You have your orders, Lycurgus hissed. In a flash, the Messenger was gone, leaving only a few rustling leaves in his wake. *Now, we must obtain the Moonstone.* The ghastly spider loomed large over Dartmoor and Rowan, and the two cowered in his presence. *Know that I am charged with one task only, bringing the stone to Cornish. Should you become bothersome, I will taste your juices.*

"How dare you! My father would never allow me to come to harm," Dartmoor shot back. "Your idle threats serve only to guarantee yourself punishment for daring to speak to me in this way!"

Lycurgus closed in on Dartmoor. *I never do or say anything by whimsy, young fool. Anger me again and even the maggots won't feed on your remains. Horrible things happen to Spriggins when they venture out into the dangerous woods, the kinds of things your kin weave into stories to tell each other at night. Do we have an understanding?*

"Of-of c-course, we do," Dartmoor stammered.

Rowan had nothing to add for the first time in his life.

This way.

Lycurgus stalked off. The others followed.

The Messenger sped through the forest so quickly that he seemed little more than a blur. He followed the pulses on the air effusing from his mistress, Queen Erebus. The dozens of orbs patrolling the trees sensed his approach and prepared for him, positioning their spinnerets. They began loosing hundreds of nearly invisible, viscous strands that formed a net among several trees. The Messenger did not break stride and plunged headlong into the web, his momentum causing him to crash to the ground. The orbs instantly descended upon him, encasing him in layers of silk. They buoyed him on their backs, cut an opening in the web wall surrounding the entire village, and marched him to the center of the village to see the Queen.

In the middle of the sacred mushroom ring, they came upon their destination, the newest addition to Willow Hills: a fortress made entirely of densely woven silk looming over the rest of the village. The building itself was made up of a cluster of spindly spires, each connected to the next by gaunt webbing resembling stretched skin. It was fortified by a menacing, spiky outer barricade crawling with no less than a hundred wolf-spider warriors, skulking about and keeping watch. The Spriggins who once relished their views of the mushroom ring now kept their blinds drawn and shutters shut to ward off the corrupting hex oozing from the perverse structure. A tumor in the heart of Willow Hills, the castle of King Cornish and Queen Glenna spread its malignity throughout the village, hollowing out the once joyous and sprightly borough and leaving it a dolorous and desiccated haunt.

The guards permitted the orbs past the main gate to take their bounty inside the palace. They scurried down long hallways and ceremonial chambers and descended below ground, coming out into an expansive prison chamber. The dungeon consisted of several cells comprised of thick webbing. These cells lined the walls, save for a break in the middle of the chamber, where there was a long and dank passageway. The Bluebells shared a cell, and across from them, on the other side of the corridor, were the new arrivals: Oden, Oakley, Sadé and Ludwig, each in their own cages. They had extensive silk wrappings on their feet, courtesy of the orbs, to prevent them from using their talons to escape. Several fearsome spiders stood watch over the prisoners.

Cornish, who had come to torment his prisoners, turned to behold the orbs bearing his long-awaited and precious cargo. "Ah, just in time. Take the Messenger in to his Queen." He waved his hand, and the orbs scuttled down the thickly webbed and foul-smelling ingress in between the holding cells. From within its depths, the prisoners heard sounds reserved for nightmares. Gwilyn and Llangollen had endured such gruesome noises before, but the owls had not. All of them blanched with horror.

Cornish turned to his captives and let out a ghoulish laugh. "Why look you so? Erebus must feed. Why do you think you're here?"

"You're sick, Nettle!" Gwilyn howled. She had lost none of her spirit, and she needed it, now more than ever, especially since her husband had been withering away, becoming more and more despondent by the hour. And in Cornish's presence, Llangollen was nearly comatose. Coupled with his injuries, he spent most of his time prone on the floor of their cell. She looked up from her battered husband. "Why do you insist on keeping us down here?"

"It is not of my doing. The Queen herself requested the pleasure of your company. She prefers her food *fresh*."

"You monster!"

Cornish scoffed at her with a muted laugh in his throat. The horrid slurping and sucking ceased, and the orbs presently returned, carrying a smaller webbed parcel, which they placed at Cornish's feet. "Cut it loose," he commanded.

The orbs stripped away the wrapping, and Cornish reached

down and held up Oscar's crown.

"It can't be!" Oden wailed, and the other owls trilled in anguish.

"Oh, but it is," Cornish said, relishing this moment. "This is all that remains of your former king and his Spriggin consort. Let it serve as a reminder to any who would dare defy me!"

Llangollen stirred from his stupor and raised his head. "If Annwyn is dead, your time will not be long in this world," he croaked. Cornish waved his hand, and Llangollen's head dropped.

"Ohh, Annwyn..." Gwilyn sank to her knees and sobbed; the thought of losing her daughter depleted her. "You can't be dead."

"Don't despair, you will join her soon enough." Cornish glanced down the wretched hallway before whisking away, leaving the owls and Spriggins to mourn their losses.

Annwyn had been walking on the path for a few hours now, while Oscar kept pace flying from limb to limb. As scary as it was from the outside, inside, the wood was nothing of the sort. They passed through the harrowing entranceway expecting to enter a realm of untold horrors, but instead found themselves in a verdant and lush redwood forest. The light was dim since there was no sun in the sky, but the wood was still inviting and comforting. The Emerald Flower had maintained a steady shine since they embarked on this trail, giving Annwyn just enough light to navigate. Then, without warning, the ring flared up, startling Annwyn and sending a pulse of light through the woods. Oscar swooped down to a branch above her head.

"What was that?"

"I don't know. Wait, do you hear that?"

"Gimmie a sec," he said, cocking his head. "It's coming from over there. I hear running water, but voices, too. I can't make out what they're saying."

"They?"

"Hold on, let me get a better listen." Oscar silently flapped his wings and disappeared into the distant branches of the canopy.

"Oscar!" Annwyn cried as loud as she would dare. She stood there, alone in a thicket of ferns, her heart pounding in her ears. She slunk back against a tree and hunkered down. She heard a sound again, but this sounded a little like splashing. Yet underneath that noise was something that filled her with morbid dread—Oscar hooting in distress. Annwyn's fear melted away, and she raced down the trail toward the commotion. The sound of rushing water got louder until it roared in her ears. She burst through the tree line, and onto the banks of a brook, where she discovered the source of the frenzy: Oscar resting in the middle of the water and taking a bath.

"Hooo, does this feel good," he hooted. "Hey, Annwyn, you should get in; the water's nice and warm."

"Oscar, don't ever take off like that again! I almost lost you once, I just couldn't bear the thought of losing you again," she welled up.

Oscar stopped splashing, and he waded over to her, remaining in the steaming waters. "I'm sorry, Annwyn. I didn't even think of that. Well, don't worry, from now on, I promise that no matter what, I won't leave you. Deal?"

"Oh, Oscar!" Exasperated and exhausted, Annwyn collapsed on a rock on the shore, putting her head in her hands and letting out a huge sigh.

"I beg your pardon," the rock said.

Annwyn shot up with incredible speed and lost her footing in the coarse sand, sending her backward into the brook's soothing waters amid a small splash. Then the rock opened up and out popped a turtle's head supported by three newly sprouted legs. Annwyn sat forward in the shoal. "Why, you're not a rock, are you?"

"I should think not." The little turtle, her eyes, body and shell a vibrant mosaic of orange, yellow and brown, extended her head to the tip of Annwyn's nose and smiled through a chipped beak. "I'm no more rock than you are from the looks of things. My name is Ellie Elderberry, Story Keeper of Babbling Brook. I spend my days here listening to the sagas of the rushing waters. And who, pray tell, are you?"

"I'm Annwyn Bluebell of Willow Hills, and this is Oscar, the Owl King."

"Well, I had no idea I was in the presence of royalty. It is my great honor to meet you both. What is it that brings you all the way out here?"

"Whew, it's a long story. I don't think we have time for the whole thing right now, but I can give you the short version."

"I have time."

"We're here because Emmlen, the Lady of the Emerald Lake gave me this ring, and it has brought us here." Annwyn held the Emerald Flower forth, and it buzzed with light.

"Well now, I've seen that ring before, I have. Hmmm, Emmlen, you say…I've not heard from her in ages, but if she has sent you, then you must have grave things on your mind. Then again, don't we all? No matter, know you have found sanctuary here."

"Thank goodness," Annwyn sighed in relief. "Ellie, something you said before, about listening to the brook and hearing their stories.

What did you mean by that?"

"Precisely what I said. If you listen closely enough, you will hear it, too." Ellie pulled her head back slightly and closed her eyes. "Ahh, there it is . . ."

"I hear them," Oscar trilled. "Those are the same voices I heard from all the way up in the trees. Who are they? And how come they're so quiet now?"

"They are the spirits from within the earth, and they come here to share their wisdom with those who choose to listen."

Annwyn put her ear to the water. "I can hear some whispering, but I can't understand it."

"Give it time child, if you are meant to hear them, they will speak to you."

Oscar heard the voices clearly, but they made no sense. "What are they saying, Ellie?"

"This may not be what you want to hear. They speak of an impending darkness crossing the land and engulfing all in its path. Even now, I can feel its approach. The days have darkened and grown cold."

Annwyn looked closely into the flowing brook. She began to hear a trickling of voices that grew into one. "Oh no!" she gasped, covering her mouth with her hands.

"What is it?"

"Oh, Oscar, it's terrible! Our people are prisoners, and there are spiders everywhere in Willow Hills!"

"Imprisoned? Spiders? What's going on, Annwyn?"

"I don't know…I can't understand them now. Ellie, what are they saying?"

"They do not speak to me about this matter; it is only for you to hear. Mmmm, from the sound of it, evil has already befallen your village, something the council will want to hear about."

"Council?"

"Why, Annwyn Bluebell, how is it you are friends with the Owl King and know nothing about the forest council?"

"Yeah, Owl King, why is that?"

"You never asked."

"A wise king, indeed," Ellie mused.

"Seems to me the wisdom skipped a generation…"

"Now, now, let's not quibble. The council meets soon to determine what to do about this deviltry menacing the forest. Oscar, I had hoped your first visit would have been under more favorable circumstances, but such is life. Come to our meeting. Tell us your tale and share the knowledge of the brook. Perhaps, together, we can make sense of this."

"Where is it held?"

Ellie hoisted herself up on her three legs and ably began walking off. "It's not too far from here, just follow me."

"Won't I be cold?"

"No, you'll find that you're quite dry once you get out, and the heat of the brook will stay with you for hours. Now, let's hurry along." Oscar and Annwyn left the water and followed after her.

Ellie led them through many tangled vines and nettlesome thickets, until they reached an alcove surrounded by ferns. A steaming pool of water sat in the center of the clearing and warmed the air around them. Encircling the pool was a series of alternating tiki torches and tree stumps, the latter serving as seats for the council members. All the animals in the forest had representation at the council, and at present, they were milling about, speaking in hushed tones: Rumors, gossip and innuendo, fueled by feverish imaginations and tales of woe, ran rampant until Ellie and her two companions appeared.

The animals all silenced themselves when the venerable turtle spoke.

"Please, take your places at the council circle. Let us begin straight away, as we have much to discuss," Ellie called out. Annwyn and Oscar walked behind the aged turtle and stood beside her stump when she took her seat alongside all the other animals. "I suppose you're all wondering who my guests are, and why I have brought them here."

"I know who that is," interjected Vivi Cloverleaf, the fox. "That's Oscar, the new Owl King. Last I heard, you were missing."

"I heard he was attacked by a Spriggin!" the jay squawked. The crowd let out a collective cry, and many of them eyed Annwyn with suspicion.

Oscar stepped forward. "Friends, it is true, I am the Owl King, and I did have a recent brush with death, but this Spriggin here saved my life. This is Annwyn Bluebell. She and I come before you now with grave news. I have been cheated of my crown, and we have learned from Emmlen that the scoundrel who took my eye is the same behind the gloom falling upon our fair wood." The council broke out in hushed deliberations at this news, and Oscar obliged them.

Annwyn leaned in, whispering, "That was pretty good."

"Thanks, who knew?"

"How do we know we can trust you? I don't see no crown!" the badger badgered.

"Yeah!" the magpie added. The jay seconded the motion.

Oscar raised his wings. "Listen, we must trust each other. It is unfortunate that my first appearance at the council has to be this way, but the danger we are facing together cannot be defeated if we are divided. Let us unite during this witching hour and take action against the pestilence plaguing us. We two before you have been tasked with its destruction, and as proof of my word, behold this, the gift from the Lady of Emerald Lake!" He motioned to Annwyn, who was not expecting this dramatic cue. She stood there, eyes wide as saucers at this sudden attention. Oscar cleared his throat, and turning his head, he spoke out the side of his beak: "Annwyn, show them the ring."

"Oh yeah, the ring." Annwyn shook the cobwebs free; she stepped into the center of the council circle and held her hand out over the hot spring. The Emerald Flower blazed to life in the rising steam, its surging power bursting forth and forming billowing vapors of jade light. This display jolted the animals, and even sent a few of the more skittish among them scampering behind their council seats. Annwyn, looking quite chagrined at the stir she had caused, mouthed "I'm sorry" a few times to the animals as they returned to their places at the rotunda.

"This is the Emerald Flower ring. Its great power will guide us on our quest to find an end to the darkness," Oscar boomed. Annwyn stepped back from the pool, and the light subsided.

The animals composed themselves, and Ellie ventured her head out: "What the Owl King says is true, friends. The brook has told stories of the Emerald Flower for many years now. From what I have heard, this ring is to be a beacon in the darkest, most sorrowful depths of despair. This ring will cut through the twilight shroud and uncover what was once thought lost, the Moonstone."

"Moonstone? That's an old fox's tale!" Vivi protested.

"Is it? Look around you. You know what's happening here in Anglia. The deposed sun brings no daylight to the land, and no moon graces our night skies. Chill winds gain strength and blow through our homelands, causing them to freeze. Some of you here tonight came to tell us of how cold your realms are becoming. Even as we speak, this pool that's always served as our source of energy is dying, soon its waters will turn brackish and foul. It will not be long before all of the forest lies under a blanket of eternal cold and darkness. There is but one thing that can stop this horrible fate, the Moonstone. It exists, and the Owl King and his Spriggin friend are on their way to find it. We shall do everything in our power to help them on this perilous journey."

The animals entered into fervent debates and heated exchanges as the weight of Ellie's dire tidings sank in. Then, unexpectedly, Phineas Duckweed, one small, green frog, leaped forward to the edge of his seat and chirruped to claim the floor. The council yielded to him, and he began. "There is a tale among my clan, and I'd like to share it. The story goes: One of our ancestors long ago protected the Moonstone. It was stolen, and he was banished to the Nether Realms where he met with a fearsome demon. Legend has it this monster stole the stone, and has since guarded it, devouring anyone who would dare enter its lair to take it. Even though most animals think the demon isn't real, there is one rumored to know its whereabouts. We frogs call him Ismene, the Mushroom King, and he is the oldest living soul in all of Anglia Forest. He can be found in Webtoe's Leap, what you all know as Fir Hollow. That's all." Phineas peeped and sat back on his stump.

"Is what he says true, Ellie?" Oscar asked.

"Indeed it is, Owl King."

"Then how do we get there?"

"Go back to the brook, and follow its easterly branch until you come to the Pebblestone Path. Fir Hollow rests at the end. The way is long and fraught with danger, but it is there you will find Ismene; he will be able to guide you further. Now, if there is no further business before the council, we must decide how best to help these two on their way. They will need more than they have presently to meet this challenge. Any resources you may have at your disposal will suffice.

Come now, let's not be stingy."

"We'll make sure they stay warm," Warren Fleetfoot, the representative of the rabbits, piped up.

"Us and the squirrels can dig deep into the stockpiles and get you some food," a plucky chipmunk named Dash chirped.

"Don't mind that cheeky chap! If you like eatin' twigs and bark-chips, they got ya covered," the magpie cawed. "*I'll* get you real food. I know where to find some of the good stuff."

"Better not be from my berry patch again, Riley Rumplefeather," Ellie scolded.

"*Better not be from my berry patch again,*" the rascally magpie mockingly mimicked.

"Enough, Rumplefeather," Hart, a hulking buck, interrupted, "dispense with the folly and let us continue with the task at hand. We can all gather provender for you, Owl King and Annwyn Bluebell. What more do you require?"

"I'm sure anything you can give us is fine. We appreciate the kindness," Oscar bowed.

"I'll go with you," a flinty voice called out. It was Vivi Cloverleaf. "I know the way to Fir Hollow better than anyone, and I've even been inside before."

"Oh boy, here we go again," Riley squawked, "can't have a meeting without hearing about that!"

"You say you've been there before?" Annwyn asked the fox, wisely deciding to ignore the mouthy magpie.

"Sure. Plus, I know all the shortcuts, too. We'll get there lickety-split."

Oscar leaned in. "Pssst, are you sure this is a good idea? Can we trust her? You know how foxes are."

"Do *you* know the way to the mushroom guy? I don't."

"Good point."

"Okay, Vivi Cloverleaf. We'll go with you."

"It is settled then," Ellie announced. "Animals of Anglia, return to your homes and gather what you can. Tomorrow, King Oscar and Annwyn Bluebell set off to seek Ismene. If no one has anymore to say," she glared at Riley for a moment, "I call this council to a close." At that, the snakes slithered, the butterflies flew, the lizards leapt, the dragonflies darted, the grasshoppers sprung, and the rest of the council members retreated along side them. After the ceremonial procession ended, Ellie, Oscar, Annwyn and Vivi were the only ones remaining.

"Well now, you'd best hurry along with Vivi before it gets too cold out here. Tomorrow promises to be a worse day than today."

"I'm starting to notice a trend here. We're prepared for anything at this point," Oscar said.

"Yes, well, I certainly hope so. Miss Cloverleaf, would you mind escorting our guests to their lodgings?"

"Course not. Come with me, you'll be staying in my den tonight. I've got plenty of room and some nice, soft straw beds waiting for you. Let's go." They started off, and the little fox let out a whistle when she got a closer look at the Emerald Flower. "You'll have to tell me all about that ring later."

"Sure thing, Vivi. Good night, Ellie."

"Good night, dear girl," Ellie showed her chipped smile again. The three of them vanished from sight, leaving the turtle to her thoughts. Now alone, Ellie looked upon the pool. It was no longer steaming, and the sadness she felt was far colder than the air around her.

CHAPTER 7

Midnight Encounters

Cornish sent the spiders to every house, for he was determined to find out who had escaped from the Fairy Circle. Screams rang throughout the tiny village as the beasts rampaged and ransacked every home. The marauders terrorized the Spriggins, and using their diabolical methods, they learned Pooka, Dandelion and Ash were missing. The spiders rounded up their families and marched them to the web fortress. They were taken down into the prison chamber where the Bluebells and renegade owls were being kept. The wolf spiders forced them into the center of the room. Gwilyn looked to see what all the commotion was about and signaled to Llangollen, who could do little more than groan. Oden, Oakley and Ludwig watched the sad procession but struggled to keep their footing. Sadé sulked in her cell.

The air chilled as Cornish emerged from the Queen's lair and sized up these pathetic wretches. He began slowly circling the group.

"Have you helped your family members escape? Think wisely before you answer this question. I will not tolerate lies." He looked more sinister now: He had dark circles forming under his jaundiced eyes, and his skin had turned an almost translucent pale. His mere presence sent those around him into an instant panic. "Answer me!"

"W-we were unaware of any plan to escape. I thought Dandelion had gone to her room for the night. I never would have let her out into such danger. Please don't hurt her. I just want her back." Tears rolled down Verbena's face. Perry was already bawling.

"Shut that child up! I cannot bear his incessant crying," Cornish sneered at Verbena.

"Perry, honey, it's okay." Verbena picked her son up, wiped the tears from his stained cheeks, and kissed him on the forehead. The way a mother's kisses always do, this pacified Perry. Poppy embraced them both.

"And you, Alders and Roses, what have you to say?"

"We didn't know. Do you think I would have risked my son? If I knew of some crazy plan, I would have put a stop to it immediately," Scarlet Rose insisted as she stepped forward, "we would simply not have allowed it." Her husband Thurston pulled her back and held her close to him. "But I hope they find a way to stop you! And then it'll be you in a cage!"

Cornish kept circling, unfazed. "Is that so? What say you, Alder

Clan? What excuse do you offer for your child's treachery?"

"I have nothing to say to you, Nettle," Abe Alder scowled. His wife Calysta clung to his side.

"Do you not? Perhaps some time down here will help you all remember how you let your children become hunted fugitives. And if I find them first, I shall not spare them the *discipline* they seem to be lacking."

He showed his teeth, turned, and with a flare of his robe, signaled for the empty cells next to the Bluebells to be opened. The orbs did their work, and the wolf spiders forced the captives inside. The orbs quickly sealed them in, and the wolf spiders returned to their posts, two of them guarding each door. Gwilyn got as close to the wall as she could and smiled reassuringly at her friends. It provided some measure of comfort that they could all see each other through the webbing.

But even Gwilyn lowered her head when Cornish spoke. "There will be no escape, only death. The Queen grows hungry, and soon she will need to feed. Consider yourselves lucky, for your demise will not be quite as horrible as the one awaiting your children." Cornish's eyes rolled back into his head, and he raised his palms out in front of him. The chamber dimmed when he began reciting a wicked incantation and plumes of thick, acrid smoke poured forth from the ground. Without warning, the room shook as if it were going to crumble altogether. The imprisoned held on to each other, unsure if they were witnessing their last moments alive. Abruptly, the earth split open, and in one swift motion, out slithered two devilish copperheads in a burst of brimstone. Their eyes glowed with a menacing red, and their bodies exuded a sweltering heat, which scorched the floor in their wake. Spitting and hissing, they circled the room, hungrily inspecting the terrified inhabitants of the cells, sending their searing tongues through the meshed webbing to taste the prisoners before returning to their master's side.

"No, my pets, I know you wish to gorge yourselves on these morsels, but they are not the reason why I called you here. Seek out the Spriggins who fled this village. When you find them, you may feast."

"You scum! If I get out of here, I'll—" Abe charged his cell door, but he just became hopelessly tangled in it. Calysta struggled to pull him free. "You'll burn for this, Nettle!" he roared.

"Will I?" Cornish unleashed a maniacal laugh that echoed in their heads. He turned his back on the prisoners and with his serpentine escorts, left the chamber.

Gwilyn faced her friends. "Don't give up hope. Our children will survive and defeat Cornish somehow. I can just feel it."

"I pray you're right, Gwilyn," Thurston spoke gravely. "We all do."

Dandelion, Ash and Pooka rested by a small fire. They had cleared the western stretch of Anglia Forest and were camped by a small copse of trees near Toadflax Gorge. After running for hours on end, they could go no further. With the invaluable assistance of the Flicker Brothers, Pooka constructed a lean-to out of lashed saplings, completed by a pine-branch roof. The meager fire they had burning was all they dared build, and it was enough to keep them warm, but not to take the chill from their bones. They had spoken briefly when they cooked their supper and put on warmer clothes, but they had fallen oppressively silent since then. Even the normally luminescent Flicker Brothers kept their tail lamps dim.

Dandelion did not look up from the fire when she broke the silence. "What do you think happened back there?"

"Back where?" Pooka asked.

"Back at the festival. We all know Annwyn didn't kill Oscar, so what happened? Did you guys see anything?"

Pooka hung his head. "No, I didn't."

"Nor I," Ash shook his. "But I don't need to see it with my own eyes to know those loathsome Nettles are the ones that did it."

Pooka's eyes flashed. "How do you know?"

"Are you kiddin'? All I know is that Oscar goes down, Dartmoor blames our girl, and the next thing you know, we're all tearing at each other's throats. But who makes it all stop? Cornish. And not by talking, neither. It's like he froze us in place. I couldn't move, could you?"

"No," Pooka said somberly, remembering that horrible night. He saw Annwyn under Dartmoor's light, stunned and terrified like a cornered, wounded animal. His was a lone voice in defending her, but the words left his mouth without a sound. If only he yelled louder, fought harder, he could have saved her...

"I didn't think so. And what's more, when it came time to choose a leader, all I could say was 'Cornish.' I would've chosen ripe manure as our king before the likes of him, yet all that came out of my mouth was his name. Why is that?"

"I don't know." Dandelion's voice was barely audible.

"It's an evil magic, it's got to be! I'd bet my left foot Cornish is using some sorta forbidden sorcery. How else would he be able to give all them spiders orders like that? Do you know any spiders who ever took orders from a Spriggin?"

"No, I guess not," Dandelion opined.

"Yeah, spiders don't do anything spiders don't want to," Flicker chimed in.

"Course not! It's Cornish and that witch of a wife of his. And don't think that sneaky little weasel Dartmoor's got nothing to do with it. I've always said those Nettles were good-for-nothin', dung-eatin' scallywags!"

Ash's words fomented the passions swirling inside Pooka, and he fought to restrain them. He had always been a taciturn Sprig, so much so that some in Willow Hills thought him aloof, yet it never bothered him, for he always sought to live harmoniously and peacefully, and if others got the wrong impression, what of it? But Dartmoor had obliterated his harmony by taking Annwyn away from him. Pooka had known for years Dartmoor coveted Annwyn, attempting to possess her, just as he had with any other trinket or bauble which aroused his fickle fancy. But she always proved too strong for that coward, and since he could not have her, he drove her away. Dartmoor. Any mention of that bitter name only served to remind him of his loss and caused a fire to burn inside him, granting him formidable power. It was this same power he unleashed to slay the spiders; if he got the chance, he would use it on Dartmoor.

"You're right, Ash, and they'll be punished for what they've done," Pooka said.

"We're with you," Flicker said, and his brothers flashed in agreement.

"Yeah! I'm ready for a little payback! I been meanin' to plant my foot in a Nettle behind for years!"

"You'll get your chance, Ash, I promise. But we can't do it alone. How do we find Annwyn?"

Ash slumped back down. "That's a tough one."

"Hey, I know," Dandelion chirped, springing to life. "Why didn't I think of this before? Jeez, it's only the reason we went to the Fairy Circle, after all."

"What on earth are you talkin' about, Dandy?"

"Our instruments! Let's play a song! If anything's gonna work, that will!"

Ash glanced at the dark woods with trepidation. "But what about the spiders? They might be out there."

"If they were still looking for us, they would've spotted the fire by now," Pooka assured him.

"Yeah, but our music'll carry a lot farther than this dinky little fire."

"We'll just have to risk it," Pooka answered. "Our whole village needs us now."

"Besides, we'll just play quietly," Dandelion offered.

"Oh, of course, Dandy, since you're so well known for being quiet," Ash nervously chuckled. I hope they know what they're doing, he thought. Ash produced the mandolin from his pack and sat, legs akimbo, resting the instrument in his lap. He picked the melody of the song Annwyn played to honor the new Owl King. Pooka supplied a sparse beat, offset with Dandelion's well-timed tambourine. Flicker, Sparky and Flash hovered in the air and flashed their lamps in time with the music. Ash switched to chords and played harder, Pooka and Dandelion increasing the tempo of the song along with him, and maintaining a singular focus: finding Annwyn.

Then the fire moved. It was barely perceptible at first, but the normal flickering and crackling of the fire grew into a flaming twister that stretched completely over their heads. The Spriggins now played with reckless abandon, their music filling the perpetual night sky. The flame tilted downward and finally rested midway to the ground, facing north. The twirling, fiery pillar pulsed with heat four times before slowly retreating back into the fire pit. The three friends ended their song, and the Flicker Brothers landed on Dandelion's shoulder.

"Did you get what you need?" Sparky asked.

"Yep," Dandelion replied.

"We go north tomorrow," Pooka stated. "Let's get some sleep. I'll take first watch."

"If you insist," Ash added.

After putting their instruments away, Dandelion and Ash unfurled their sleeping bags and nestled in under the shelter. The lightning bugs doused themselves and found cozy spots among the fresh pine boughs comprising the roof. Transfixed by the flames, they were all soon asleep. Pooka sat down next to the fire and smiled at his exhausted friends. Let them sleep, he thought. He would be the only guard that night; he wouldn't rest again until he found Annwyn.

Dartmoor and Rowan had been following Lycurgus for days now, and they were growing weary of it. The giant spider never needed to rest, and whenever they did stop to camp, he watched the Spriggins with the same motionless gaze he used to stalk his food, causing them to sleep with at least one eye open. It did not help matters that the sun had not risen since they left, and the woods had grown increasingly frigid to the point where they could see their breath when they exhaled. And since the days consisted of little more than walking in the cold until it was time for rest, it came as a shock to the Spriggins when Lycurgus halted in his tracks during a trek through the northernmost section of Anglia. The Spriggins' arachnid steeds followed their master's example and came to a standstill.

"What's this, now?" Rowan barked. "Why're we stoppin'? We ain't even at the Meadmallow Grasslands yet. I thought we were supposed ta get ta the mountains, and this ain't helpin'!" Lycurgus unnerved Rowan, and this sudden change in behavior spurred a dozen horrible fantasies in his head of the spider making a meal of him. Unfortunately, his natural response was to run his mouth.

Keep your trap shut, halfwit, Lycurgus bristled. He slowly turned around and faced the Spriggins. *Son of the Steward, continue along this path to the Moonstone. You know where it is to be found, so make haste in obtaining it. I have other matters to tend to.*

"Other matters? What could be more important than finding the stone? My father won't tolerate deviance from the plan."

This is no deviance. I have sensed a presence that requires my attention. The Owl King and his sidekick have survived, and are now making their way north.

"What? That's impossible! How could the owl still be alive?"

It seems not everything worked as it should have. Regardless, I have sensed them on the air, and your father wishes for me to make use of my talents and dispose of them. He feared they might yet foil our designs, so I will hunt them down and ensure they are never seen again. Make your way to the stone. I will find you when my business is completed.

Dartmoor's neglected conscience acted up. "But, must you kill them both? If we do away with the Owl King, then there's no need to kill the girl."

Lycurgus twitched a forelimb. Dartmoor's mount bucked him free and sent him sprawling in front of the giant spider. Lycurgus fell upon Dartmoor and cradled his face to within a hair's breadth of his fangs. *Did I not warn you earlier about questioning me? I will kill three Spriggins today, if I see fit.* He stabbed Dartmoor in the shoulder with the tip of a fang and slowly edged it forward, searing through his flesh and despoiling his blood with venom. Dartmoor convulsed; foam formed in the corners of his mouth and spilled out over his chin to punctuate his moist, intermittent screams. Lycurgus jabbed Dartmoor in the chest with a prickly forelimb, knocking him to the ground with a dull thud before disappearing into the woods to embark on his evil errand.

Aghast at the monstrous spider's brutality, Rowan scrambled to be free of his own mount, afraid he might be next. He tumbled to his feet and rushed over to his injured friend. "Dartmoor! Hey, Dartmoor, you alright? Damnation, yer bleedin' too much!"

"Don't touch me!" he howled, casting Rowan aside with a swift forearm and knocking him down. He stood over Rowan, thick streams of blood coursing from an angry and pulsing wound. "We've work to do!"

Clutching his erupting shoulder, Dartmoor limped to his spider and mounted, leaving dark pools of blood behind him; his life dripped down the sides of his spider. Nevertheless, he took the reins and snapped them, sending his mount striding into the gloom. Rowan watched in disbelief as his friend darted off, leaving him alone in the woods.

Pooka remained on watch, determined to protect his friends. He was propped up against a log close to the fire, and fighting off sleep, when something rustled just outside his range of vision. Pulse rising, Pooka rose from the fire, crawled to the lean-to, and grabbed his drum. It might come in handy.

"Guys wake up, something's out there," he dared to whisper.

No luck. Dandelion and Ash continued slumbering, and even the lightning bugs didn't stir from their beds. He heard a twig break and the distinct sound of footfalls. Pooka decided to confront this intruder on his own terms. With a hand poised over his drum, he stepped into the frigid darkness and crept toward the source of the disturbance. It was pitch black, but Pooka used the noise to guide him, and the crackling and rustling continued, growing louder with each step he took. Heart now racing, he tapped his drum slightly as a warning -- any spider out there would know what his drumming could do. But then, the sound stopped. Without anything to follow, Pooka was at a disadvantage in the dark. He took half a step and froze in place. He could feel the breath of the stalker on his face.

"Hello," a tender voice said.

"Ahh!" Pooka stumbled backwards and dropped his drum, which landed awkwardly and tumbled away from him. He scrambled over to it and picked it up, positioning it for a strike. "Show yourself! I'm warning you!"

Flicker and his brothers suddenly arrived and landed on Pooka's chest, their behinds dimly glowing.

"What's going on Pooka? We heard you yell. Are you okay?"

"There's someone behind you," he whispered.

The three daring lightning bugs spun around, took to the air, and flooded the immediate area with as much light as they could squeeze. There, standing right before them, was a small white-tailed deer.

"Who are you? Why are you here?" Flicker commanded, sounding as imposing as a lightning bug could be expected to.

"Sorry to scare you so. I am Ama. I have been searching for you, and now, thank goodness, I've found you."

Pooka kept his hand poised over the drumhead. "Searching for us? How is that?" Who else knew they were in the woods besides the spiders?

"Allow me to explain. The forest has eyes and ears, and friends of mine spotted you. Word got back to my herd, and here I am."

"That still doesn't tell me why you're here."

"Yeah," Flicker butted in.

"I'm here to help. I recently attended a council of all the forest animals, and we had two unexpected visitors, the Owl King and his consort, Annwyn Bluebell."

"ANNWYN!" Pooka exploded. "She's alive!"

"And quite well, all things considered. She and Oscar told us all about what happened in your village, and when the birds started singing about a group of Spriggins wandering in the woods, I decided to investigate. I'd like to help."

Ash and Dandelion emerged from the darkness and stepped into the ring of light, rubbing their eyes and yawning.

"What's all the yelling about?" Ash crankily uttered. "Hey, who's this?"

"I'm Ama, I'm a friend."

"She knows where Annwyn is!"

"You do? Where?" Dandelion blurted out.

"I know she and the Owl King make their way to a wise being in search of answers. His name is Ismene, and he resides far from here in a place called Fir Hollow. If you were to continue on foot, you would not get there in a month."

Dandelion shook the last of the sleep from her head. "Oscar? He's alive?"

"Yes, he came close to death, but he survived thanks to your friend Annwyn."

Pooka's brow knitted. "How do we find them?"

"I will call my herd, and we will take you to see Ismene. He will tell us how to find them and the Moonstone."

"The Moonstone?" Ash waved a dismissive hand. "That only exists in legends. Kids stuff."

"No, it is real." Ama moved closer to Ash and Pooka. "And Annwyn and the Owl King are in search of it. We need only reach Fir Hollow, and all will be revealed."

"Why can't you take us to Annwyn?" Pooka insisted.

"Annwyn is at least a day ahead of us, and she might have already visited Ismene," Ama said. "I would not know where else to find them if that is the case."

"Who is this Ismene you keep mentioning? How do we know he can help us?" Ash grunted.

"Ismene is the Mushroom King, the oldest and wisest being in the forest," Ama replied. "His name was known only by select members of the Woodland Council, and few others before now, but secrecy is a luxury we can ill afford. He knows things long since forgotten by *trees*. When we reach him, we will find your friends."

"Then we go there." Pooka's word was final.

"Can I make a suggestion?" Dandelion yawned. "How about we get some more sleep before we go to see this mushroom?"

"That is an excellent idea, Miss Dandelion."

"Hey, how'd you know my name?"

"I know who you all are. Remember, news travels fast through the forest. Please, take your rest tonight. We set out tomorrow, and word is a wicked storm's blowing in. You will need your strength for the journey ahead."

"Ama, won't you come join us by the fire?" Pooka asked, extending a hand to her.

"It looks inviting, but I must prepare my herd for the trip. I will return in a few hours. Until then, sleep well." Then, with white tail flashing, Ama darted into the night.

"Goodbye," Dandelion called after her.

With the lightning bugs in the lead, the Spriggins returned to their camp. Dandelion and Ash quickly found their bedrolls, and they soon entered a snoring contest with each other. Flicker and his brothers resumed their places in the pine branches. Pooka sat up with the fire, still on watch, now even more hopeful of seeing Annwyn again. He leaned back against the log and watched the gentle dancing of the flame swaying with the wind.

After being abandoned by Dartmoor, Rowan had finally managed to saddle his ride again to search for his friend, but once he grabbed the reins, the spider took off, zigzagging though the forest and leaving the Sprig nowhere near in control of the jaunt. The beast darted this way and that, directly into low-hanging limbs, poisonous vines and jagged underbrush, skillfully avoiding these hazards itself while concurrently allowing them to batter, bite and tear at the Spriggin in the hopes his bungling passenger would lose his grip and be sent crashing to the ground. Incensed by the Spriggin-nectar spilt earlier by Lycurgus, the spider almost went mad with bloodlust, but it was forbidden by its leader, upon pain of death, to harm its rider. However, if this one accidentally broke its neck during a nasty spill, then there would be no need to refrain from feeding on him, since it was a cardinal rule amongst spiders never to waste good juices, especially a delicacy like Spriggin, even if this one looked gamey and sour. But so far, he had proved far more resilient than he looked.

Even had Rowan been aware of his mount's foul designs, he would not have been able to hold on any tighter. Skin bruised and pulpy from the arboreal beating he suffered, Rowan nevertheless clung to the reins with white knuckles, his hands chafed and oozing from the grip. The blood seeping onto the spider increased its fervor, and it picked up speed while bearing down on even more hazards of the wood. Finally, Rowan gathered the strength to yank on the reins to bring the spider to heel, but it didn't heed him at all.

"Stop, ya furry varmint! Blast yer hide! STOP!!!" Abruptly, the spider gripped the ground with the spiky hairs on its legs, bringing them both to a skidding halt. The sudden stop ripped the reins from Rowan's hands, and he tumbled headlong into the brush, screaming until he hit the ground hard with a loud *FUMP*. The wolf closed in on him and exposed its fangs in anticipation of devouring the Sprig, but no luck, he had survived. Disappointed, the spider backed off and let Rowan get to his feet. "Why, ya stinkin' swine, I'll—"

"Always the fool."

Rowan turned, and there was Dartmoor, casually approaching him from a shadowy corner of forest. "So, what's th' big idea?! This'un here's been runnin' roughshod all over these blasted woods, an' I got no idea where you been!"

From atop his spider, Dartmoor shook his head, sneering at this groveling worm. The bleeding from his shoulder had mostly stopped, but his arm hung limply, and dried, cracked blood speckled his cloak.

Festering corpuscles lined the garish wound, and they poked out from the tattered and frayed robes he wore. Dartmoor had made no effort to dress his injury, so he'd been seeping thin trickles of blood, but his spider knew better than to try to make a meal of this rider, no matter how much fluid poured over him. Lycurgus' venom coursed inside this one, spoiling its juices and guaranteeing a violent death for any who tried to taste them. Dartmoor continued his advance.

"We'll ain't ya gonna answer me?"

"I've been watching your antics, Rowan. We have serious business to tend to, and you're out having fun, instead."

"Yeah, it's been a real hoot! 'At spider tossed me! Somethin' ain't right wit it! I don' care what you say, I ain't getting' back on that thing! It'll be the death a' me! And what's wit' you takin' off and leavin' me back there, huh? You know I don' know where we're goin'!"

"Why? Were you scared?"

"Heh, not half as scared as you were when Lycurgus took 'at chunk outta ya."

Dartmoor dashed Rowan to the ground with a swift backhand.

"Mention that again, and I'll leave you out here for your spider. Now mount up, you wretch. We've got to clear the forest." He stalked off.

Rowan sat up and tasted blood. With the eyes of an abused animal, he watched Dartmoor leave him behind again. He nervously approached his spider, which was hungrily twitching at the sight of the blood running down his chin, gingerly climbed into the saddle, and gave himself over to the pernicious caprice of the monster, which resumed torturing him with its whirlwind pace. What did it matter? Death would be a welcome reprieve.

CHAPTER 8

Winter of Discontent

It had grown bitter cold during the night, and the first few snowflakes had begun to fall. Earlier, Annwyn, Oscar and their new host Vivi Cloverleaf emerged from the wily fox's den to an amazing sight: The sun had risen. Yet its rays did not warm the land. Dark and baleful nimbostratus clouds swooped in and blotted out the sun, causing the pall of the forest to morph from pitch black to a dull gray. And with the arrival of this harbinger came an increase in the snowfall, punctuated by shards of ice. Undaunted, they found their way to the head of the Pebblestone Path and set off through the tempest.

After traveling on the trail for a few hours, the punishing weather began to take its toll on the three companions. Annwyn began the trek with vigor, but now she walked slowly, her energy sapped by the bitter chill, and the supply-laden pack she toted on her back did not help matters. Even one of her gifts from the animal council, a rabbit-tuft coat, could not keep her warm. Oscar had puffed his plumage to help him stay warm, but the wind blew hard, and he felt tiny icicles piercing his feathers. Vivi felt winter's bite despite her fur; she shivered a little to produce some warmth, but it quickly dissipated.

"I've never felt a cold like this before. I'm freezing my tail off out here," Vivi yipped.

Annwyn cleared the snow off a fallen tree and sat down. "I just need to rest for a minute," she said, obviously winded. She dropped down onto a log and removed her knapsack. She blew into her cupped hands and wiggled her fingers to regain some feeling in them, but felt only a few fleeting tickles before they were numb again.

"Maybe we should all rest," Oscar said. He landed on a branch above Annwyn and continued to puff out his feathers, while Vivi huddled close to Annwyn and curled her tail around her nose. "Annwyn, let's see what there is to eat."

"Sure." Annwyn opened the bundle. Though relatively small in size, even for a Spriggin, the pack held many more items than it should have, thanks to some special engineering by the chipmunks. She removed a parcel filled with a mixture of nuts, dried fruits and oats and spread it out on the log. Oscar alighted next to the food, and the three of them ate eagerly, not realizing how much the cold had deadened their appetites. Annwyn tried to focus on the pleasant inner warmth she felt from the mix, but she could not.

"What do you think is happening at the village?"

"I don't know, Annwyn. I just hope everyone is alright."

"I can't even wrap my mind around what's going on. Just look at our forest. It's dying." She could no longer hold back the tears, and they trickled from her eyes for just a moment before freezing on her cheeks.

Vivi poked her head out. She reached up and lapped the salty crystals from her face before they had a chance to fuse with her skin. "Don't cry, Annwyn. Dangerous."

Annwyn smiled thinly and petted Vivi's head. "Thanks for the advice, but all I want to do is cry anymore. Everyone expects me to do all these incredible things, but can I really? Doesn't all this seem impossible? I just want to lie down and let the snow cover me…"

"Don't talk like that, Annwyn! You've got no reason to doubt yourself. Heck, if it weren't for you, I'd be dead. Look how far we've come, all the things we've done. I couldn't have done any of it without you, and I can't think of anyone else who I'd rather save the world with. Emmlen gave you that ring for a reason, Annwyn, and before all this is done, you'll show us all why."

"I hope you're right, Oscar."

The little fox nudged her arm. "I'm with you till the end, Annwyn."

Annwyn scratched the fox behind her ear, eliciting a few rapid kicks from her back leg. "I guess we won't get any closer to Ismene by sitting here." Annwyn forced herself to stand, repackaged the rations, shouldered the pack and bundled herself in her coat, tightening the belt and hood. She tucked her hands in the pockets and with one last shiver, continued down the Pebblestone Path. Vivi skirted in front of her to resume the lead, and Oscar kept to the trees. None of them spoke. They had said enough already.

Little did the unsuspecting group know Lycurgus crept ever closer, stalking in the shadows with a thirst for blood burning inside him, his hairs twitching from vibrations on the wind. Even with the interference of the falling snow, he could feel them more intensely now, and knew they couldn't be too far away. He squealed with delight when he came across their tracks in the snow. He examined them and saw that a third must have joined his quarry, a fox. The giant spider rubbed his palps over his fangs at the thought of tasting fox; he would feast well when he caught them. He followed their footprints, but the snow began to fall even harder, and his clear trail quickly vanished under a blanket of white. Undeterred, Lycurgus pressed on, fighting the elements.

Asio draped herself over her husband to keep him from succumbing to the cold. A few owls formed a barrier around Otus, while the others huddled around the base of the mushroom. The worms told them snow had begun to fall in Anglia, something that had never happened before. But the owls lost contact with the worms, for the ground had since frozen. The webbing confining them to the amphitheater was effective at keeping out the snow, but not the icy winds. Every passing moment was a struggle for the owls. Ever since the Spriggins escaped, the spiders doubled their numbers inside the amphitheater and cut the owls' rations in half. Without nourishment, Otus's condition had worsened, and his breathing became increasingly shallow. He barely clung to life. Now he opened his eyes and looked upon his wife.

"Asio," he sputtered, "my love, I have something to tell you."

"What is it?" She drew close, her face only inches from his.

"I'm not long for this world."

"Don't say that! You can't leave me, just hold on a little longer, you have to!"

"I wish it weren't so, but it is. Even now, I can feel the venom eating away at me. Soon, I will be with my fathers in the Great Sky. And I will be watching you, love. I will always be with you and our son." Otus's eyes grew intense, and his voice dropped even lower: "Our son is alive, and he will be back soon."

"Oscar's alive? How do you know that?"

"Though part of me still exists in this world, my soul is departing for the spirit realm. Already I can see beyond the confines of this life. And I see our son." At this, Asio began bawling. "Now is the time for you to be strong. Oscar will need you before this is all over. He is alive, Asio. He will return."

"Please, Otus, don't go," she sobbed, clinging to her husband.

"We will not be parted for eternity; someday you will join me among the clouds. But my time has come. I love you, Asio, and I will always be with you . . ." he trailed off, and with his final bit of strength, Otus leaned forward and kissed his precious Asio. Then, he was gone.

"Oh, Otus, no!" She laid her head on his chest and wept. The owl sentries turned around and stared in disbelief at the sight of their beloved leader, dead. They and the rest of the owls could no longer contain their pain, and they joined their queen in grieving.

The skies turned even more brutal, and the snow pelted Oscar, Annwyn and Vivi. Oscar was braving the treacherous winds, and swooping from branch to branch, when he felt a great sadness wash over him. So great was the anguish, he faltered on his next landing and crashed to the ground. Annwyn rushed to her friend with Vivi right behind. He looked pained, if not necessarily from his fall.

"Oscar, what's wrong?"

"Something terrible has happened."

"What?"

"It's my father, I can't feel him anymore."

"What do you mean?"

"He's gone."

"What? How do you know? Maybe it isn't true, Oscar. It's just...you're just scared is all."

"No, Annwyn," Oscar struggled through his tears, "it's a bond that all living Owl Kings share. Even when we're apart, we can feel each other inside. But in my heart, where my father was, now, there's nothing."

"Oh, Oscar, I'm so sorry." Annwyn held her friend close and let her tears flow, despite the frigid temperatures. Vivi approached them and nestled up against them, offering what comfort she could.

Oscar wiped his eyes and stood back from his friends. "I will find who did this and avenge my father, mark my words. I don't care what happens to me now. All that matters is finding the Moonstone so we can expose the source of this evil and kill it."

"Oscar, are you okay?"

"I have to be, Annwyn. I am the Owl King of Anglia Forest, and my people need me now. My sorrow will have to wait. Vivi, how close are we to Ismene?"

"Just a little farther to Fir Hollow," she answered. "We'll be there within the hour."

"Good, let's go then. Lead on, Vivi."

"This way," she said, and after rising and shaking loose the coating of snow she'd accumulated, continued down Pebblestone to even deeper forest despite the wintry gale. Oscar resumed branch-hopping while Annwyn, holding her coat tightly around her shivering frame, plodded through ever-deepening mounds of snow. As they marched, the storm mercilessly battered them, but its torments were no match for the pain in their hearts.

Dandelion, surprisingly, woke before Ash. It was not actually light out, but the darkness had lifted somewhat, making it seem more like dusk. She sat up and rubbed her eyes to find a multitude of deer grazing around their campfire in a shower of flurries. She emerged from the lean-to, let out a mighty yawn and popped a few bones in a protracted stretch. "Morning, everyone."

Pooka was sitting on Ama's back. "Hey, Dandelion. Just taking a riding lesson."

"Looks like fun, do I get to try?"

"Of course." Ama whistled, and a petite doe with large black eyes came bounding over. "Dandelion, meet Grace."

Hi, my friends call me Dandy."

"Dandy it is," Grace smiled. "Climb aboard."

"Ooh, gimme a sec. I'll be right back." Dandelion went back over to the lean-to and kicked the still-slumbering and snoring Ash in the butt. "Hey! Get up, we get our own deer!"

"Mmmhph! Whazzat?! Dandy, what in blazes are you doing?!" Ash snarled.

"It's time to get up and meet your deer."

"Sometimes I wonder if I wouldn't be better off with the spiders." Not content to let anyone sleep, Ash shook the roof of the lean-to, causing the Flicker Brothers to crawl out of the pine branches, more than a little crabby.

"What's the big deal?" Flash grumbled, stretching his antenna and giving his butt a test-flash. "It was warm in there."

"Well, it's cold out here, so get up and join the rest of us in misery," Ash grumbled right back. He dragged himself from his bedroll and plopped down in front of the fire. He looked up with puffy eyes. "I'm up now, so who's my deer?"

"I am," a commanding voice proclaimed. Ash spun around and beheld a majestic 14-point buck. "I'm Hart, good morning."

"I'm Ash. Nice antlers you got there."

Hart eyed the Spriggin's spiky hair. "Likewise. Now that we are all here, we should break camp and be on our way. We will need to make great haste for there's talk of a great storm coming. These few flakes are but a warning."

"Okay guys, you heard him. Let's get packed up," Pooka said, jumping down off Ama.

Ash patted his tummy. "My belly's over here tellin' me a different story."

"Me too," Dandelion whimpered. Her stomach rumbled at the mere thought of food. "We'll have time to eat before we go, won't we?"

Dandelion's growling gut suddenly reminded Pooka of his own hunger. They had eaten little since their escape from Willow Hills, and he knew they wouldn't get very far in this weather without something to fill their bellies. "Hart?"

"Very well, but I advise we ready ourselves for the journey first."

Pooka patted Ash on the back. "Fair enough, let's do it."

The three of them gathered their belongings and broke down the shelter. Then, they sat by the fire and toasted some pumpkin bread and apple slices. When they finished breakfast, they doused the fire and undertook the last few tasks before they could leave. Dandelion was double-checking their provisions when she heard something. The wind picked up and carried with it a mystifying sound, an ethereal, mournful dirge.

"What's...does anyone hear that?"

Ama cocked her head to the side to listen to the wind howling through the trees.

"They are the spirits of the forest, and they talk to those willing to listen. They speak of a profound sadness, a terrible loss," Ama somberly channeled. "No, it can't be—" The whole herd froze in place. The Spriggins inched toward her. Dandelion broke the silence.

"What is it?"

"King Otus is dead, murdered."

Pooka clenched his fists. "Murdered! By who? Who did this?"

"A baneful spider, one whose heart knows only hatred."

"I can't believe it, I can't!" Dandelion cried. "They're wrong! They have to be!"

"No, Dandelion, they're not," Hart responded gravely.

"Why are all these horrible things happening? Why?" Dandelion sat and cradled her knees; this latest doleful revelation unleashed a torrent of sorrow that had been welling up inside the young Spriggin since the fateful events of the Owl King Festival, and it swept over her, causing her body to shake uncontrollably as she wept.

At the sight of his dearest friend in such agony, Ash felt a knife plunge into his heart. He embraced Dandelion and eased her sobbing.

"I don't know why, Dandy. I don't know." Pooka knelt beside them, lowered his head and shared a moment of silence in remembrance of the great King.

Hart was the first to speak: "The death of Otus is a wound our souls will carry forevermore. These dire tidings do not bode well. I never thought I'd live to see the King of Owls slain, and by a spider no less. Evil is afoot in our wood, and we must move swiftly, for time is slipping away, and our peril is greater than we thought."

"He's right," Pooka said, standing, voice steeled with resolve. "We need to get to Ismene, so we can find Annwyn and Oscar. Let's stop this madness now before it's too late." He put a reassuring hand on Ash's shoulder and one on Dandelion's. They rose and faced the deer. "We're ready."

"Move out," Hart ordered. The three friends grabbed their meager belongings and saddled the deer. The lightning bugs remained stashed in their friends' hoods, hidden from the bitter cold, and the group dashed off quickly into the murky woods.

Dartmoor and Rowan rode single-file through the northern forest. Rowan's mount had long since given up on eating its passenger, since it could not risk expending too much energy with the temperature dropping so precipitously. He'd live, for now. Enough snow had fallen that it packed under its own weight and allowed the spiders to walk on top of it, making for a much smoother ride (especially for Rowan) than before. They had traveled without speaking for an interminable time before Dartmoor broke the silence.

"The old fool is dead. He got what he deserved."

"What're ya talkin' about?"

"Otus is dead. Lycurgus's venom did its job." Dartmoor attempted a laugh, but it devolved into a hacking cough, and he yanked his spider to a halt. He tried to quell the spasm, but it raged inside of him, causing him to convulse and choke. His agonies culminated in a stream of thick, bloody vomit which burst out of his mouth and showered the snow with a gory spray.

"Hey, Dartmoor, you alright?"

"I'm fine!" Dartmoor shot back. "Mind yourself!"

"Just askin'," Rowan mumbled under his breath. "How d'ya know the owl's dead?"

"Don't worry about it. I just know," Dartmoor gnashed his teeth. "No more questions! We must hurry to find the Moonstone." He turned his mount to face Rowan, and Rowan was shocked by what he saw. Dartmoor's face was pallid, his veins visible under his thinly stretched skin. His lips were cracked and tightly drawn over his bloody teeth. But the worst were his eyes: They had turned yellow, and the skin around them was black. They burned in Dartmoor's skull and bore a hole through Rowan.

"Dartmoor, what's happenin' to you?"

"Nothing you need concern yourself with! Just do as I say!" He spun back around and spurred his spider forward, deeper into the storm.

Pooka, Dandelion and Ash bounded through the forest. The woods had grown lighter, but the flurries gave way to a heavy snowfall that quickly enveloped everything in a sheet of white. The rapid accumulation slowed their progress somewhat, but with the help of the swift and tireless deer, they still managed to make their way to the southwestern trailhead of the Pebblestone Path. Hart led the herd, followed closely behind by Ama and Grace. A sizable number of deer flanked them while smaller groups of scouts splintered off and kept alert for danger.

"Here it is," Hart called out. "If we can keep this pace up, we should be there in half a day." The herd thundered forward.

Little did they know, they had an even greater obstacle ahead of them, for the unnatural vipers weaved though the woods, tongues tasting the air for the scent of the hunted. The pounding of the herd's hooves made it even simpler to track their prey, and they zeroed in on them. Even the frigidness could not stop Cornish's cold-blooded killers since their preternatural body heat precluded their freezing to death. Indeed, the snow on the ground melted in advance of them, allowing them to move unfettered through the harsh weather. They slithered virtually undetected toward the deer, the only hints of their presence being their glowing red eyes since the driving snow quickly concealed the melted paths they forged and the icy trails left in their passing.

As Hart galloped, he noticed one of his scouts pull up alongside him, on the other side of the tree line, and begin to flash his tail frenetically. That meant only one thing: predators. But what could it be? Even the wolves and mountain lions would have sought refuge long ago in these conditions, and most of the other potential dangers in this region were scavengers, not exactly the type of menace a healthy and unified herd needs to worry about. If something was out hunting them during this storm, the threat was truly a grave one. Hart halted and reared up, causing Ash to hold on tight to his neck. The whole herd stopped behind him. Ama's ears perked up, and she raised her white tail. Grace and the other deer instantly froze and tensed up, readying themselves for sudden flight. The Flicker Brothers peeked out. The only sound was the patter of snowflakes dashing through the trees and onto the ground.

Pooka dared whisper, "What is it?"

"Danger."

They held still, enduring the terrible tension and waiting for a sign of their stalkers. They did not have to wait long as, just in front of them on the trail, one of the gargantuan copperheads broke through the brush and lashed out at Hart with a massive hiss. The big buck sidestepped the strike, but Ash nearly toppled off. "Hold tight, young Sprig!" Hart yelled. He stomped his foot, and the herd turned in unison to run back down the trail. Behind them waited the other demonic snake, coiled and ready to strike. They were trapped, and the snakes bobbed and weaved, fangs uncovered and devilish eyes hypnotizing. The deer stood motionless, but facing outwardly, so that at least one pair of eyes was always watching their attackers. They lifted their tails in a sign of alarm.

"What should we do?" Pooka asked Ama, but no answer came. Pooka looked to his friends. Ash gripped Hart with white knuckles, and Dandelion sat without blinking or breathing. Hart snorted and stamped a back leg. The smaller bucks slowly worked their way to the sides of the herd so they were directly facing the underbrush. All of the deer quivered in anticipation.

Without warning, the snakes lashed out, striking forward and hissing, causing a panic amongst the deer. At this moment the bucks charged, heads down and leading with their antlers, and the snakes barely escaped being trampled. The bucks tore through the brush, creating new paths to the open wood, and the herd split into three groups: Hart led a contingent directly up the trail, while Ama and Grace broke to the left, and another group went right. One of the snakes bolted after Hart, and the other sped toward the two does.

Ash got a bad feeling, so he looked behind him; there was the hellish copperhead, winding toward them with freakish speed, the heat from its infernal flesh liquefying the snow in its wake. Wisps of oily smoke poured from the fiend's nostrils, and its fangs promised a potently painful death. Its red, hateful eyes were locked onto him.

"Hart! One a' those things's right behind us!"

"Hold on!"

Hart wagged his tail, and the remaining bucks with him burst through the brambles, taking the rest of the deer with them. Now it was just Hart, Ash and the snake on the trail. The snake nearly made a meal of Ash when Hart looped around a tree and jumped over its head, narrowly missing its slashing maw. The sheer force generated by the jumping buck launched the traumatized Spriggin into the air for a brief moment, and it was no small miracle that he slammed right back in the same position, though he did have the wind knocked out of him, making him hyperventilate. It was all Ash could do to hold onto to Hart with the world spinning like it was. Mindful of his winded and weakened passenger, Hart slowed to a complete halt and turned to face his opponent in a small clearing. The pit viper turned as well, coiled to strike and emitting a horrid hiss that cut through the already wailing wind.

"What are you doing? Let's get out of here!" Ash wheezed.

"No, I'm going to end this. Do you have the strength to hold on?"

"I'll try."

Hart paced back and forth, sizing up the snake. In an impressive display, he began bucking and kicking up snow, his nostrils blowing out snarls of smoke. Ash turned ashen and gripped the buck even tighter, praying for deliverance. Then, Hart lowered his head, pointed his antlers forward, and barreled towards his adversary. The snake leapt at the big buck, but Hart was too quick for it; he impaled the snake on his antlers and thrashed his head violently, breaking the snake's body. Despite the searing pain bolting through his rack from the beast's burning body, he threshed harder, until the snake stopped flailing. He flung its limp carcass into the brush.

Ash loosened his grip and fell off the deer, landing next to the bloodied corpse of the snake. The serpent's head twitched involuntarily and its mouth snapped aimlessly as its last unholy breaths left it, causing Ash to yelp and scramble away. He took shelter behind Hart. "Gaia's eyes! Hart! It's still alive!"

Just to placate the Sprig's fears, Hart walked over to the slain devil and poked it with his antlers. It didn't move. "Not to worry, my friend, it's dead."

"I can't believe it. I thought we were goners for sure. I've never seen anything so terrifying."

"This was no normal snake, Ash. This was a demon conjured from the realm of shadow. Yet that wasn't the first of those beasts I've had to fight, and it won't be the last. The other serpent is still out there. Come on, we need to find it and destroy it before your friends come to any harm."

These words slapped Ash in the face and shook loose his incredulity. Hart lowered himself and the Spriggin jumped up onto his back. They sped back down the path, all the while watching for a sign of the other snake. A few bucks and three does entered the path in front of them at full sprint. They flitted their tails.

"What's going on?" Ash hollered.

"It's the other snake. He's after your friends!"

"We've got to help them!"

"Hold tight!" The deer in front of them sharply turned right off the trail, and blazed through the woods. Hart and Ash followed.

The stinging cold, being jostled and bucked on the back of a charging deer and the very real prospect of taking a bone-shattering spill to the ground at any moment paled in comparison to the horror Dandelion experienced when she worked up enough courage to turn around. Normally fearless to a fault, the one thing in the whole world which could cause Dandelion to wilt with dread, without fail, was snakes. She still had nightmares about a garter snake that once surprised her when she turned a rock over in search of pill bugs. What she saw now guaranteed a lifetime of sleepless nights.

"Grace! Don't look back! Just keep running! Oh no, it's gonna catch us! Faster! Go faster!!!"

The little deer pushed herself even harder, but the deepening snow, coupled with the whipping winds, prevented her from keeping pace with Ama and the rest of their faction of the herd. The slithering monster lunged forward, scattering the deer so that they splintered and disappeared into the deep wood. Without the added safety of numbers, the serpent closed in on its target, the two Spriggins. Ama took the lead and Grace kept up as best she could, but they were losing ground to the snake slicing through the snow. Pooka turned around and his heart sunk; Dandelion and Grace were seconds away from succumbing to the gaping maw closing in.

"Ama, we'd better do something and quick!"

Using her peripheral vision, Ama sized up the situation, and the deer knew instantly what to do. She slowed for a moment to let Grace and Dandelion pass her, and when the copperhead lunged, she struck it in the face with a sharp hoof. The snake momentarily fell back in pain, and Ama quickly regained her full speed despite her scorched foot. She cut hard to the left while Grace continued running forward, hoping her gambit would pay off and allow the others to escape while the viper chased her. A contingent of bucks anticipated Ama's stratagem and laid in wait just ahead on the trail, ready to run this demon through as soon as she passed them. But the snake knew it could not readily catch the wily doe, so it abandoned this chase and turned its sights on easier game—the small deer and the terrified

Spriggin. In a flash, it was gone.

"Ama, he's going after Dandelion and Grace!" Pooka bellowed. Ama swerved and rushed after the snake, which already gained on their friends.

Grace ran as fast as she could, but she couldn't outpace the deadly predator. The snake pitched forward in one swift movement and grazed Grace's hind leg with its formidable fang. She crashed to the ground, throwing Dandelion off her back and onto a thicket in a soft, but thorny, landing. The snake immediately homed in on the dazed Spriggin. Dandelion slowly opened her eyes, and there, above her, loomed the monstrous serpent, mouth agape and fangs glistening with venom. It relished the moment before the kill and let out a debilitating hiss. It struck at her, but Dandelion fell through the bush and onto the ground. The snake passed over her, came back around, and slithered its head into the undergrowth for the kill. Dandelion kicked at its groping mouth, the soles of her boots charring from the continued contact.

"Help! Help!" she shrieked.

All of a sudden, the snake started convulsing and writhing. Dandelion scurried from underneath the brush and saw Ama on the other side, trampling the snake. Pooka was by her side, beating it with a club, which began smoking and turning black. Soon the copperhead's body lay still, leaking putrid blood into the ground. Ama immediately plunged her hooves into a bank to ease the pain from the snake's skin, the snow instantly melting and sending wisps of steam into the air upon contact. Pooka dropped his charred weapon, ran over to Dandelion, and hugged her.

"Are you hurt?"

"No, he didn't get me," she said panting, still a little dazed and covered with scratches from the briars. Her eyes widened. "Where's Grace? Grace!"

Flicker came out of Dandelion's hood and signaled to Flash, who left Pooka's cloak. They looked around for the little doe. They found her collapsed in a snowdrift not too far away. There were flecks of blood around her.

Ama approached her. "Are you okay Grace?"

Grace moaned a little as she extended her back leg, revealing the thin incision from the fang. "Uhh, I'm fine, it's just a scratch."

Ama inspected it. The viper's tooth cut deep into the young deer's leg, but the intense heat from the creature's blistering temperature cauterized the wound, miraculously preventing any major loss of blood.

"You're lucky, it doesn't appear he injected any venom. Can you walk?"

"I think so." Grace grunted a little and managed to get to her feet, though she wobbled and limped severely. She tumbled over and winced in pain. "Maybe not."

"Hold on, I've got just the thing," Dandelion said. She produced a packet of healing herbs from her pack and mixed them with just enough snow to give them a gummy consistency. She applied a thick coating of the unguent to the wound and wrapped it with her scarf. "There you go, Grace. That'll heal you in no time. Go ahead, try it out."

The little deer hesitantly drew herself up with her forelegs, expecting to feel the crippling jolt of pain as soon as she shifted her weight to her injured hind limb. But that didn't happen. In fact, she felt no pain at all; her leg was sturdy and sure, almost better than it was before the snakebite. "Wow, thanks, Dandy. I feel great! Get on, I'm okay to ride." She lowered herself, and Dandelion climbed on. Pooka got back on Ama while the two lightning bugs nestled into their Spriggins' hoods again.

"Alright, let's head to the meeting spot," Ama ordered. "We don't know where that other snake is."

"I wouldn't worry about him." It was Hart and Ash, striding toward them behind a buck and three does. They came to a stop. "Looks like you all handled this one," Hart said, eyeing the trampled snake.

"Dandy! Pooka! I'm so glad you're safe."

"You didn't think a little snake was gonna get us did you? We're just too good," Dandelion laughed, stroking Grace's neck.

Pooka gave his friend a nod. "Glad to see you, Ash. So, Hart, what's our next move?"

"The three of us will continue up the path."

"What about the rest of the herd?" Ama asked.

"I'll send these scouts here with word to the others that they should regroup at the meeting spot, and then fan out into the woods in their patrol groups. Apparently, someone knows where we are and wants us dead. We'll move faster as a small group, and with any luck, we'll get to Ismene before this storm makes the way impassable." Hart dispatched his scouts and turned to the others. "Follow me, the trail's up ahead."

Hart and Ash bounded up the trail with Ama, Grace and their Spriggin passengers right behind them.

"Pebblestone ends just ahead. We're close to Ismene, now," Vivi barked over the howling wind. They came to the end of the trail and looked down upon a grove of trees at the bottom of a small hill. "That's Fir Hollow." Vivi sniffed the ground but got mostly a snout full of snow. "I can't get a good scent, but that's where Ismene is."

"I'll meet you guys down there." Oscar swooped as best he could through the snow and attempted to land on one of the outer firs of the hollow, but as he came in for a landing, he barely grazed one of the limbs with an outstretched foot when the needles pierced his skin, sending an excruciating pain unlike any he had felt before up his leg. He cried out in agony and tumbled back into the air; he regained his balance and found a safe perch on a nearby dogwood, favoring his left leg while the throbbing subsided in the right. Annwyn and Vivi heard him screech and tumbled down the hill through the heavy snow out of sheer panic. The frantic Sprig spied Oscar in the tree, wincing as he attempted to put weight on his wounded foot.

"Oscar, Oscar, what happened?" Annwyn asked breathlessly. "Are you hurt?"

"No, I'm okay, but a word of advice – don't touch the trees."

"Oh yeah, I forgot to tell you about them," Vivi said.

"You knew about this?"

"Yes, but I didn't think about it. I don't have wings, you know. Besides, you're not the only one they've stung, I've got a scar on my nose from them!"

"I'll give you a scar—"

"Hey guys, this is no time to argue. We need to find a way inside," Annwyn mediated. "Any ideas?"

"I found a secret entrance by accident once -- that's how I got my scar thank you very much -- but I always forget where it is. You'd think I'd remember with all the times I come here, but nooo. Well, that's a magic grove for you. Just hold on, it's around here somewhere." Vivi leveled her nose to the ground again and sniffed; her tail twitched excitedly, and she started skirting back and forth at the base of the trees. "Aha! Here it is!" She dug under the snow until all that was visible was her tail. She stopped in front of a certain tree and gave a muffled yip through the snow. Directly above her, the trees' limbs parted like welcoming arms, brushing aside the snow (and Vivi) and presenting an open path into the hollow. Vivi's head popped up from the newly created snow bank. "In we go."

"How'd you do that?" Oscar queried.

"Uh-uh, a fox has to have her secrets. After you."

Annwyn stepped into Fir Hollow. Oscar flew in and landed on the ground right behind her, followed by a trotting Vivi. The tree limbs closed behind them, sealing the entrance. Annwyn and Oscar were astounded by what they saw. No snow fell inside this grove of firs; in fact, it was warm, and sunbeams cascaded through the boughs. Annwyn looked up and saw the bluest sky she had ever seen. The ground was covered with a dewy moss and several clear, tinkling streams crisscrossed in front of them.

"It's nice, isn't it? I like to come here when I need some me-time," Vivi said.

"What is this place?" Annwyn marveled.

Vivi sidled up to her. "According to lore, it's a place outside time. It was here before the forest sprouted, and it will be here long after it's gone, that's what all the stories say at any rate. I don't know about any of that, I'm just glad there's no snow."

"I'm with you on that one," Oscar said, shaking the last icy droplets from his feathers. "Ah, that's better. So, where to Vivi?"

"One of these streams will lead us to Ismene."

"Which one?"

"I don't know."

"I thought you'd been here before."

"I have, many times. It's just that I've never found Ismene in here. He's kind of hidden."

"Seriously, nothing's easy," Oscar sighed.

"Give me a second. Maybe I remember something about how to find him. What did my grandmother used to say? Something about a flower or something . . ." Vivi trailed off. She got up and started scouting and sniffing.

"I guess I'll get comfortable," Annwyn said. The warmth from the sun was too much for her in her rabbit-tuft coat, so she removed it. When she put it on the ground, she felt a slight tug on her right hand, and the Emerald Flower started glowing. "Hey Oscar, it's happening again."

"What?"

"The ring, it's pulling my arm." She held her hand aloft, and the ring glowed even brighter.

"That's it!" Vivi came jumping over, panting with excitement. "My grandmother used to say that only a shining flower could light the way to Ismene. I never had any idea about what she was talking about, but Annwyn, it's your ring!"

"Here we go again," Oscar said.

He and Vivi got behind Annwyn as she followed the pull of the Emerald Flower, though this time, the ring was not really leading her as it had before; gone was the almost violent tug Annwyn had reflexively resisted. She paused on the path, her anxious companions stopping behind her. It was a subtle shift, but Annwyn felt the ring's power slowly seeping into her, poised, awaiting her command. Annwyn exhaled deeply and her mind cleared. She reached out to the ring, and it welcomed her; the ring was no mere magical item, it really *was* alive! Her consciousness and the ring's intertwined, and she willed it to find Ismene. As Annwyn did so, she and the ring moved in unison, a feeling of déjà vu washing over her—somehow, somewhere inside her, she had already found the place they needed to go, and she only needed to take her friends there.

They came to a creek that was deeper and swifter than the others. Annwyn lowered herself to the water, and she dipped her hand below its surface. Instantly, the creek sparkled with green light, shining and twinkling like the facets of a gem.

"This must be the one," Annwyn smirked.

She got back to her feet and began walking with the flow of the stream, the others following just behind her. They forged ahead. The tree cover grew thicker and thicker, blotting out the sun, but the light from the Emerald Flower made it navigable. At last, they broke through the tree line and came into a small, brightly-lit grotto. The creek they were following cut through the mossy ground and spilled into a steaming pool surrounded by ferns, a few scattered rocks, and a downed log.

"Hello, Ismene?" Annwyn called. "Where are you? We've come a long way and need your help." No reply.

"Don't tell me he's not here," Oscar groaned. "I guess the ring was wrong. C'mon, let's go back."

"No, this is the place," Annwyn replied, "I know it is."

"Maybe we should go."

"Maybe you should stay." A voice came from over by the pool, startling them.

"Who's there?" Annwyn peered at something curious. "Hey, look."

She noticed a small mushroom, sporting a red cap with white

spots, suddenly grow out of the side of the log. It inflated like a balloon until it popped off and fell to the ground. Two tiny arms sprouted from its sides, and the mushroom tried to right itself, but not with a great deal of success.

"You over there, would you mind giving an old chap a hand?" it spoke, voice muffled by the ground. Annwyn and Vivi rushed over and helped the little creature sit up on his base. There, in front of them, was a mushroom no bigger than a bumblebee with a jovial face and smiling green eyes. He had thick, mossy brows and chin whiskers. "Thanks for your help," he winked. "It's tricky trying to stick that landing."

"Are you…"

"Oh, my apologies. I am Ismene, humble servant of Anglia Forest. You must be Annwyn Bluebell. And I assume this is the young Owl King? Your highness, it is a great honor to meet you." He attempted a bow and nearly toppled over, and he would have too, were it not for the intervention of Annwyn and Vivi. Ismene looked over the fox. "Who is this, now?"

"I'm Vivi. I'm the one who brought these two here. I hope you don't mind."

"Ah yes, the one who's always snooping around in my grove," Ismene chuckled. "No, of course I don't mind, Miss Cloverleaf. I'm actually rather glad you finally found me. Good conversation is quite hard to come by around here, and I always enjoy a pleasant visit. Please, won't all of you sit?"

Annwyn and Vivi did just that near the warm pool, while Oscar alighted on the downed tree. Ismene didn't so much walk as float over to a patch of moss, next to the lip of the pool, and plant himself.

"How did you know our names?"

"This is not the first I have heard of you or your friend, Owl King. I am the keeper of all the history of the forest. I know all that happens within its borders, and even some things that do not. I have known for quite some time you would come seek me out."

"So you know why we're here," Annwyn said.

"Yes, you come to me about finding the Moonstone, and find it you must. But be warned, as perilous as your travels have been up to now, they will only worsen the farther down this path you go. Yet, if you don't obtain the stone, then we will all cease to exist."

"What do you mean?" asked Oscar.

"A greedy and power-hungry Spriggin has tapped the realm of dark power in an attempt to realize his own selfish dreams. But unknown to him, he has unleashed a potent and malevolent force which has been waiting ages to wreak havoc once again."

"Who is it? Who has done this?"

"You know who it is. It is the same foul being who robbed you of your eye, endangered Annwyn's life, and the lives of all who reside in your beloved Willow Hills."

"Cornish," Annwyn whispered. "It's Cornish."

Oscar's good eye narrowed. "Then he's responsible for my father's death, too. I'll pay him back in blood!"

"Oh no, young Owl King, do not surrender to those base desires. That is how Cornish lost his way, and now many are suffering because of it, you most of all. Your desire to see justice done is admirable, but no good can come from a thirst for vengeance. Your father knew this. He was a great king, and one of the finest rulers Anglia has ever known. And I know the wounds in your soul feel like they will never heal, but keep this thought close to your heart: your father watches over you and will never truly leave you."

"I know you're right, Ismene, and I won't betray my father's legacy. But there will be blood."

"Very well, Owl King. Cross the Meadmallow Grasslands to the Barrows at the base of the Jawbone Mountains. Follow the narrow dirt path up through the mounds to the Witch's Hands. You will know them when you see them. From there you must descend into the underdark of Devilkin Mountain. Find your way down to the underground lake. It is there the Moonstone lies hidden."

"How hidden?"

Ismene let out a little sigh. "It is deep inside the belly of a terrible demon."

"*Inside* a demon? How are we supposed to get it out of there?"

"Well, there's only so many ways into a demon's belly. I'm sorry I can't tell you more, but prescient as I am, there are some things I cannot answer. Now that this evil has been unleashed, confusion has replaced certainty in my mind. It has brought this storm upon us, but the worst is yet to come."

Annwyn sat forward. "What is it? What are we facing?"

"It is known by many names, but in Anglia, it is called the Maelstrom, and it is more than just a storm. The cold and snow I have kept from my sanctum is but the beginning. Soon they will cease and give way to. . ."

"To what?"

"The end," he whispered, "the end of us all. Cornish Nettle foolishly released this dark force upon us all in an attempt to harness it for himself. Others before him had tried the same, and one-by-one they all fell victim to it. Yet Nettle was different, he found a way to channel it. But once the Maelstrom was released, it began to gain in strength. It rages out of his control, and if it is not stopped, it will consume existence."

"No, it won't," Oscar said with a steely resolve, "we're going to get the Moonstone and send this thing back to the Nether Realms."

"How are we going to do that? How can we stop something that can destroy the world? No one even knows what the Moonstone does."

Ismene popped out of the ground and floated over to her. "True enough, Miss Bluebell. There are a great many mysteries in life, like the one you wear on your right hand."

"The ring?"

"The same. When Emmlen gave you that gift, you did not know what to do with it. You doubted yourself and despaired. And yet here you are, in my grotto. You discovered in yourself the power to use it, and when you find the Moonstone, it will be the same. But there is something Emmlen did not tell you. That ring and the Moonstone belong together. They were once used in tandem to bestow peace on Anglia, but they were separated long ago, when the Maelstrom first crept into the world of light."

"Wait, you know Emmlen?"

"Quite well, too. She and I have been acquainted for as far back as I can remember, and that's a pretty long time, that is. Why, who do you think's been nudging you all along? It's not a coincidence you're here, you know. You were a little lost before, so the ring and I gave you a little push in the right direction. After that, you did just fine on your own, though you may not have known it. Besides, we've done this sort of thing before, ages ago and with another lass named

Bluebell, no less, so take some comfort in knowing that."

"But Emmlen told me the Matriarch of my clan tried fighting the Maelstrom and failed. How do you know that it'll be any different this time?"

"I don't." Ismene's frankness surprised them. "It is true that the Maelstrom proved too powerful for her to destroy completely, but you know only part of the story. Would you like to meet her?"

"Meet her? How can I do that? That's imposs--" But suddenly Annwyn knew how.

The ring.

There they were again, tendrils of energy reaching out to her, waiting. She clasped them eagerly, and gave the command: "Take me there." A green haze seeped into her periphery, and it slowly spread, encompassing and immobilizing everything around her, the slight swaying of the forest, the steam from the pool, even her Oscar and Vivi; they were all frozen in place. The energy finally settled over her like a wispy veil, and she stood. Ismene rose along with her.

"Don't worry, my dear, your friends will be fine. Now it's time to take the next step."

And so she did.

Annwyn reached out with her mind and parted the veil. Beyond the opening she saw a world of muted, swirling colors, which became more vivid and began to take shape the closer she came to the aperture. With Ismene beside her, she stepped through the portal, which felt to Annwyn like slowly submerging in cool water, and found herself on the shores of the Emerald Lake.

The world was vibrant, everything shimmering with a bloom of light so bright Annwyn had to squint. Soon her eyes adjusted, and she saw an Emerald Lake unlike any she had ever beheld before. Gone was the oppressive haze, the simmering menace, the creeping dread. It was a sheet of limpid green glass, the blue sky crystal clear, sunshine beaming down upon her. Warm, inviting, nourishing.

And on the water's edge stood a beautiful, solemn stranger whom she instantly recognized.

"Oh my, is that..."

"Olwynn Bluebell, a Spriggin of great importance and your ancestor," Ismene finished for her.

"But, she looks so troubled, so lost... Why is she so sad? Olwynn! Olwynn!" she called out, but the figure made no acknowledgement.

"She cannot hear you, Annwyn," Ismene said. "You may visit times that are not your own, but you have no power to change what you see, no matter how much you may want to. You would do well to remember that."

Some of the glint left Annwyn's eye. "But look! She needs my help!"

"She is beyond your help. What you will see here today has already happened, Annwyn. It may not look like it, but this is no more real than the stories you heard as a child."

"So I can't talk to her? Never know her?"

"Look inside yourself, and you will find you already know her. We have not come to talk. Look up."

At that, Annwyn raised her gaze to the sky, and the once sparkling sky had begun to turn upon itself, curdling into a gnarled fist of pulsating, black clouds. The wind began howling and whipping, and the air turned frigid. Annwyn was shocked she could feel these things; if this was only a story, how come...

A horrid shriek filled the air, freezing Annwyn with dread, and she saw the swirling, black clouds begin to form a demonic face a thousand times more terrifying than any beast that had ever haunted her nightmares. A wind funnel that looked like a loping, slathering tongue formed and began to race toward the Spriggin still staring forlornly into the Emerald Lake.

"Olwynn! Look Out!" Annwyn cried.

The tongue raced toward her, but Olwynn Bluebell did not seek cover; she began chanting, and a green light flared up around her, growing in intensity with her voice. Just as the tongue reached her, intent to pull her into the maw that awaited above, she split the air with the crescendo of her chant, raising her arm and sending a powerful pulse of green energy from the ring she wore on her right hand. The emerald column met the tongue, burning it into nothingness, and it streaked toward the horrid visage in the sky, blasting it into oblivion with a crack of thunder that threw everyone to the ground.

Annwyn lifted her head, still dazed, and witnessed an all-too-familiar pall creep over the Emerald Lake. Through the haze, she saw the lifeless form on Olwynn Bluebell on the shore, waves gently lapping against her, with a meager trickle of light emanating from her ring, Annwyn's ring, the Emerald Flower.

"No, no, no, Olwynn!" Annwyn dragged herself towards her, but waves suddenly appeared, continuing to grow stronger, enveloping more of Olwynn with each gentle surge, until finally, she was gone. A tear streaked down Annwyn's face as she saw a faint green light wane into nothingness beneath the water. She buried her face in the sand, sobbing, when Ismene brushed her cheek.

"It's time for us to go back."

The veil lifted.

When Annwyn raised her head again, she was back in the grove with her friends, who were reanimated, and just as she had left them.

"Annwyn," Oscar gasped, "why are you crying? What happened?"

Annwyn told Oscar and Vivi what she witnessed, and then turned on the little mushroom. "You said that was no more real than a story!

How come I could feel everything? The wind, the earth trembling, the explosion? I feel like part of me is gone...with her. What happened to me back there?"

Ismene furrowed his brow. "I-I'm not entirely sure, Annwyn. I've never seen timewalking affect anyone like that before. I will have to think on this. But it was still just a story, and is it that unusual to be moved by a story? To have it seep inside you and fill your soul? We all form bonds with the tales that connect to us, and for you, I'm afraid, this story was more personal than most."

"It just hurts so bad."

"I am sorry, Annwyn, but mere words could not prepare you for what you face, and I don't want your story to end like hers. You have seen the Maelstrom, what it can do, and what needs to be done to stop it. Olwynn battled it with only the Emerald Flower, and she sacrificed herself to banish it to the realms of shadow and darkness. But what you saw was only the aftermath. She fought the menace alongside the rightful owner of the Moonstone, but he lost his life, leaving her alone. She entrusted the stone to a guardian who hoped to hide it, for fear it would be corrupted and bring the Maelstrom even more power, but the guardian came under a terrible curse. After that, no one knows what happened to him, even me. Reunite the Moonstone and the ring, and you will have the power to destroy this scourge, once and for all."

"I pray you're right," Oscar said.

"As do I. The Maelstrom has come to have its revenge by destroying the land in a deluge of ice and fire. Hope is not lost, though, for if you do bring these powerful artifacts together, you might just fulfill the last part of the prophecy."

"Last part?" Oscar hesitantly offered. "All the other parts are so horrible, I don't think I want to hear this one."

"Understood, Owl King, but know that in the time of the Maelstrom's return, the rightful rulers of Anglia will rise, and they will destroy this blight and restore harmony and peace."

Annwyn finally stirred at this. "At least we have one of the rightful rulers," she said, motioning to Oscar, "but where are we going to find the other?"

"Perhaps you already have, Annwyn Bluebell. You and the Owl King are linked by bonds greater than friendship, and when the two of you bring those treasures together, that which was once concealed, will be revealed."

"Graybeak's feathers! I don't know why all this stuff always has to be hidden. Emmlen couldn't tell us about the ring, or you...we've had to wander through all sorts of forsaken places just to end up here, which we could've done a lot sooner if someone would've just been straight with us. Instead of running around the woods, I could've saved my father!"

"I understand your frustration Owl King, but some things are important to discover on one's own. Imparted knowledge is a gift, to be sure, but one becomes wise only through experience. Emmlen told you what you needed to know, as have I. The Fates are not random, capricious forces, and I mourn your father's loss as deeply as any, but had you been back at the Fairy Circle with him, you would have shared his tragic end, and then all hope would be lost."

Oscar wrestled with Ismene's words, and he could not deny their veracity; he knew his father's death was not his fault, he knew things could not be any different than they were now, but no epiphany could ease his woe. There would always be a splinter in his mind, a sharp pang of different possibilities and better outcomes. He made to speak, and the others waited anxiously for his reply, but none came. Oscar closed his beak and settled himself; talking about this anymore wouldn't accomplish anything. If he wanted to set things right, it would take actions, not words, to do it.

Taking note of the owl's demeanor, and judging him placated, at least for the moment, Ismene floated back over to the side of the pool. He inspected his three guests and noticed how they all appeared drained, depleted, and it pained the little mushroom to see them this way.

"I dare say, we have dwelt on doleful topics for too long, and I hate to see such sad faces. What kind of host would I be if I sent you off in such a state? Let us remember there is always hope for a better tomorrow. That doesn't mean tomorrow will be worth a lick, but at least there's hope. And speaking of better tidings, Annwyn, did I see a pouch on your belt?"

"Uh, yes, it's where I keep my flute."

"A flute? Why didn't you say so? Would you mind regaling us with a melody? I do enjoy music so."

"Shouldn't we get going right away?" Annwyn asked. "I mean, we have so much to do, and so much depends on us."

"My dear child, rest for a spell with me. Time does not pass in Fir Hollow the same way it does in the rest of the world, and you cannot leave here with so heavy a heart. I have always found the best way to dispel the doldrums is with some music. Please humor this old mushroom and play a song."

"Don't be so modest, Annwyn, you know you're the best flautist in all of Anglia. Why do you think you were picked for my coronation?"

"Oh please, Annwyn," Vivi pleaded, "I've never heard you play."

"Well, okay, I guess." Annwyn crossed her legs and took her flute from its pouch. She held it to her lips and played her favorite song, her grandfather's melody. The sweet tones filled the grotto, and soon they began to feel the weight of the world lift from them. So great was the feeling of calm, it wasn't long before Oscar and Vivi fell into a deep sleep. Even Annwyn wasn't immune; her eyes grew heavy, and her melody grew weaker and weaker, until she stopped playing and lay down on the soft bed of moss, her flute gently coming to rest in her lap.

"Sleep well, my friends."

Ismene looked on them lovingly before retiring to his fallen tree.

CHAPTER 9

The Demons of Devilkin Mountain

Cornish sat on his throne in the audience chamber of the web palace enraptured, eyes rolled back into his skull, palms raised, and his body effusing tendrils of wicked energy. His mind raced across time and space to make contact with his son. The room rumbled as he spoke with a dissonant, otherworldly voice: *Dartmoor, Lycurgus has informed me the Owl King yet lives. Make haste to Devilkin Mountain and retrieve the stone. Do not think being my son spares you any torment should you disappoint me, boy.* Cornish produced a pitiless, gurgling giggle and woke from the trance. Eyes rolling forward in their sockets again, he gazed upon his precious Glenna, sitting in her throne as though the palace was built around her. His voice regained its normal timbre.

"They are almost there, my dear."

"Excellent," she grinned. "I was wise to chose you all those years ago, love. Yet, I sense a disturbance. This should be a time of jubilation, for our designs are working better than we expected, but you seem troubled. What is it that bothers you?" She saw a moment of fear cross his face, a sure sign of weakness, yet her expression did not change despite her rising ire.

"I'm not sure, my dearest, but I feel as though the Fates are turning against us. My grip on the Maelstrom is not as strong as I hoped it would be. Even now I can feel it slipping..."

"What?!" Glenna hissed. She rose sharply from her throne and struck Cornish across the face, drawing deep, thin cuts that seeped blood instantly. "See to it you do not let the prophecy come to fruition, for I will make you suffer untold agonies before it swallows us all! Now leave me, mongrel!"

Cornish skulked out of the chamber, using his hand to staunch the bleeding. Once in the hallway, he banged his sopping fist against the wall, leaving a splattering of blood. "How dare she treat me this way! I was the one who discovered the power! I was the one who brought it under control!" he fumed, thin strands of bloody spittle slinking down from his snarling mouth. His anger overwhelmed him, so he barreled down to the prison chamber, dragging his gory hand along the walls. Most of the sentries had been called away for other duties, and he passed the two remaining guards outside the main entrance. The Spriggins and owls stiffened when he entered, retreating to the corners of their cells at the approach of this twisted creature.

"You pathetic fools!" Cornish bellowed. "I'd kill you all now if I could!"

"What's stopping you? I thought you were all-powerful," Gwilyn dared. She was cradling Llangollen, who had suddenly seized up and could barely move. "Could it be that the mighty Cornish Nettle doesn't have the courage? You're really brave to come down here and frighten us while we're in cages!"

"SILENCE!" Cornish made a rapid crossing motion with his hand, as if he were swinging a sword, and Llangollen, ripped from his wife's embrace, slammed face-down onto the floor.

"Llangollen!" Gwilyn cried, retrieving her whimpering husband. The owls and the other Spriggins grew restless, anger supplanting their fear.

"And to think I once deigned to have my son marry your murdering daughter," Cornish sneered.

"You maggot!"

"How long do you plan to keep torturing us like this, Nettle?" Thurston shouted.

"Oh, don't worry, it won't be much longer. For when everything is ready, all of you will have the honor of being the first offering to Erebus. That's right! She will partake of your juices, and your suffering will be great. And once she has had her fill, my power will be complete!" He let out a menacing laugh and stalked off, his maniacal howls filling the halls and chilling the souls of the prisoners more than any dank dungeon ever could.

Scarlet, who was in the cell right next to the Bluebells, peered through the webbing and saw Gwilyn hunched over her husband. "How is he?"

She looked up with tears in her eyes. "I don't know." She hugged him close to her, and something startled her. She started sifting through Llangollen's dreads.

"Gwilyn, what is it?" Scarlet's voice was tinged with panic. The other prisoners all clamored to see what was happening from their limited vantage points.

Gwilyn stopped probing under Llangollen's thick blanket of hair, and a look of horror contorted her face. "There's something here, something *alive.*" She grimaced when it squirmed.

"Talk to us, Gwilyn," Abe's voice grew louder.

"Mommy," Perry simpered. Verbena pulled him close to her without saying a word. Sadé hooted nervously in her corner, and the other owls shifted restlessly from foot to foot. Llangollen's moans filled the chamber, causing the tension to rise to an unbearable level.

"Hold still, honey," Gwilyn cooed, kissing her husband's forehead. Her face tightened in concentration, and she reached her hands under Llangollen's mat of hair. She planted her foot on the wall, and in one swift motion, yanked as hard as she could. She fell onto her back from the force, and there on her chest, legs wriggling, was a bloated tick the size of a melon. "Got you, you little blood sucker!"

The Spriggins and owls recoiled in horror at the sight of the grotesque, bulbous parasite struggling in vain to gain its footing. Gwilyn jerked upright and threw it to the floor where it just sat on its back, multiple legs still twitching.

Llangollen sat up enough to rest on his elbow. He rubbed his neck with his other hand. He looked to Gwilyn with confused eyes. ""Uhh, wh-where am I? What happened?"

"Oh, Llangollen," Gwilyn gasped, throwing her arms around him and kissing him. "You're safe now, sweetheart."

"Safe? What's going on?" He gazed around with a lingering, vacant look. "Thurston, Scarlet? Is that you?"

"Yes friend, we're here," Thurston replied. "It's not just us, either. The Alders and Buttercups are also imprisoned, along with a few brave owls who helped our children escape. They're seeking help while we languish down here."

"I can't believe—AHH! What is that?!" he cried, pointing to the teetering tick.

"That was attached to your neck, dearest," Gwilyn said, petting his head to soothe him.

"How could I have not felt something so big?" He paused while something shifted inside his head. He scrunched his face and shook his head back and forth. "Hmmm, I feel different now, like I was trapped underwater, but now I can breathe. It's still a little hazy..."

"How much do you remember?" Thurston asked.

"I remember the festival. I remember the tragedy and those vile Nettles accusing my daughter of murder. The last thing I can see is Cornish over top of us in the Fairy Circle. And now I'm here. Even still, it feels like I've been asleep for a long time."

"It's that tick," Oden hooted. "We owls have come across these before on our patrols. They lurk on the outskirts of our kingdom, and if they pierce your flesh, they do more than suck blood, they can control your thoughts. Eventually, they will completely drain your life. They only grow that large right before the kill; you were lucky, Llangollen."

"Dartmoor," Llangollen seethed. "He put that filth on me. I just know it. He tried to steal my daughter. Never in a million years would I have even let him near Annwyn, and yet he convinced me to allow their union. I can't stay down here! I've got to find her!" Gwilyn helped him to his feet. "How do we get out? Oden, can't you cut through this junk?"

"No, the spiders wrapped our talons, and the webbing's too sticky to bite through. We'd just get tangled."

"I'm sorry, honey, but we're stuck here," Gwilyn intoned.

"Are we?" he said, more to himself than to her. He glanced around his cell and looked at the tick, still floundering on its back. The tick and its exposed, sharp proboscis. "Hmmm," he mused, stroking his beard.

Ismene emerged from his log to find Annwyn, Oscar and Vivi still slumbering.

"Good morning my friends, time to rise," he called out. Oscar's eye popped open. Vivi raised her head, let out a toothy yawn and stretched.

Annwyn sat up and rubbed her eyes. "Mmmm, how long have we been asleep?"

"Not too long," Ismene said. "But long enough, I hope, to shake the weariness from your bones."

"You know, I do feel pretty good, all things considered," Vivi said in between a few scratches.

"Excellent. Won't you have something to eat? You will need your strength." Ismene waved his hand, and three leaves sprouted from the ground around the pool, each unfurling and revealing a breakfast befitting an owl, fox and Spriggin, respectively.

Oscar jumped down from the log and dug in. Annwyn and Vivi followed his example, albeit with a bit less aplomb. After breakfast, the leaves retracted, and they set about preparing for their journey while Ismene watched.

"Okay, we're ready," Annwyn said, slipping her coat on. "How do we get to Meadmallow from here?"

"Hold on, I have something for you." Ismene reached inside the log, pulled out an oversized (for him, anyway), folded-leaf package, and presented it to her.

Annwyn handled it somewhat warily. "What is it?"

"A gift. Inside are special leaves. Mix them with water. It makes a lovely little drink I like to call seven-league tea. Just a few sips, and it will grant you tremendous speed. You'll be able to run seven leagues in the time it would take the swiftest forest animals. The Meadmallow is no small distance, and once you leave here, it won't be long before the Maelstrom reaches full strength."

"How long do we have?"

"A day, maybe two. You will see when you leave here that the storm has ceased, and the snow's already melting. That means it's almost ready."

"For what?"

"Fire. It will fall from the sky and leave all of Anglia ablaze, razing it until there is nothing left but smoldering earth. But if you succeed in your quest, then that won't happen, will it?" Ismene winked and gave a chuckle.

Annwyn let out a sad laugh: "No, I guess it won't. Let's get going then. Thank you for everything, Ismene."

"Oh, no need to thank me. Now, for your directions: When you leave here, just follow the stream that brought you here to the Meadmallow. But be careful, my friends, you are not the only ones who seek the Moonstone. Dartmoor Nettle is on his way to the mountain now with his lackey."

Annwyn's eyes narrowed. "Dartmoor, I should have known."

"Alas, I sense another, greater danger lurking the woods…a hulking demon…scorching hatred… I can see it only in small pieces, though it is doing its best to hide from me. Whatever it is, if it finds you, it will kill you, all of you."

"I won't be stopped. I will see justice done for my father, even at the cost of my own life."

"Oscar, no—" Annwyn gasped.

"It has to be this way, my father deserves no less."

The truth wounded Annwyn, but its sting was no worse than the other slings and arrows she had already endured. Sadly, only a dull ache throbbed inside her at the thought of losing Oscar. Her whole life she had felt things so intensely, almost intuitively, but no longer; as is true for all who've suffered greatly, her soul had grown calloused and her emotions felt separate from her, like a thick webbing she could not hope to claw through was slowly choking her soul. So be it.

If her friend were to die, she was prepared to share his fate.

"You're right, Oscar. You're right."

At that, Oscar spread his wings and took off into the trees. Vivi let out a whining yelp and followed after him. Annwyn started to follow the stream, but turned around and laid her eyes upon Ismene. He smiled reassuringly, and she left.

"I hope Emmlen was right about her," he opined, sinking back into his log.

As they reached the edge of the Meadmallow Grasslands, Annwyn took Ismene's gift and knelt down at the creek they had been following since leaving Fir Hollow. She opened the package, revealing a mound of moist, brownish, musty-smelling leaves inside. Vivi peeked over her shoulder. "Yuk, we're supposed to make tea out of those? I'd rather drink dirty bath water!"

"From the looks of it, you might get a chance to," Oscar teased.

"We need something to mix them in," Annwyn countered.

Vivi caught a whiff of squirrel in the air, and where there were squirrels, there were discarded acorns. And around these parts, the acorns came in one size – jumbo. "I'll be right back." The crafty fox fell back into the forest, rooted around some trees for a bit and rustled up an acorn cap the size of a soup bowl. She trotted triumphantly over to Annwyn with her booty. "Here you go."

Annwyn took the cap and dipped it into the cool water. She added some leaves to the cup, picked up a twig, and stirred the brew. Miraculously, the libation began heating up, causing it to bubble a bit and send steam into the chilly air, and the dank odor of the leaves transformed into a sweet aroma, like the first whiff of freshly baked cinnamon bread coming out of the oven. Annwyn stopped stirring, lifted the cap and took a sip, her tongue tingling with the robust flavor.

"Well?" Vivi asked.

"It's good, reminds me of warm June nectar." Annwyn quaffed the concoction and delighted at the taste of the tea, which was more like a thick, spicy cider. Immediately, her body warmed and her head swam a little from the jolt the beverage provided. She let out a satisfied *ahhh* before offering some to Oscar. She held the acorn cup to his beak. "Ready?"

"Bottoms up," Oscar replied, and Annwyn titled the cap backwards in unison with the owl's head. He took a large gulp and sounded a delighted *mmmmm* as it went down. Annwyn pulled the cup away, and Oscar let out a contented burp. "Wow! That's great!!!"

"My turn!" Vivi yipped. Annwyn laid the cap-bowl down, and

Vivi lapped at the tea, slurping up every last bit of the intoxicating potable. She raised her head, a little dazed and licking her chops. "Yummy! Is there any more?"

"No, that's it," Annwyn smiled, patting the fox's head.

The initial swell from the tea subsided, and the three of them sat for a few passing moments, wondering what might happen next. "I don't feel any different, do you?" Oscar asked, watching Vivi and Annwyn for a sign.

"Not really," Annwyn replied.

Then, deep inside of them, a tickling grew until it permeated their entire bodies, causing them to buzz like the wings of an armada of hummingbirds all flapping at once. The sensation of being pulled from their physical forms overwhelmed them, as if their minds had become puppeteers and their bodies, marionettes, and a dizzying feeling of floating supplanted their normal senses, somehow disorienting and familiar at the same time. Abruptly, Oscar beat his wings a little and Annwyn and Vivi began pumping their legs, and they bolted forward, unable to halt their sudden, incredible momentum. With each movement, they felt themselves effortlessly covering great distances across the wide-open swath of the veldt. They propelled themselves so rapidly, the sea of grass and snow that was the Meadmallow seemed to slow down disproportionately, elongate and slide backwards as they bounded ahead. They tore through the grasslands, appearing to the unaided eye as a blur causing everything in their wake to tumble and sway as though a gale had just blown through.

Lycurgus had the three in his sights just as they vanished into the grasslands with uncommon speed. He gave chase, but he could no more overtake them than he could the wind. Yet, Lycurgus was not dismayed, for the craven pit which spawned him granted him unnatural powers, powers he had used before to bring down greater marks than the ones he currently sought. By escaping his clutches here, they only delayed the inevitable. He called upon the dark forces that sustained him and prepared himself. The Owl King and his friends would be his soon enough.

Oscar, Annwyn and Vivi made short work of the grasslands. The vertiginous swirl of the magical tea waned, and soon the Meadmallow ceased sliding backwards; the three friends felt the full heft of their bodies return. The world finally caught up to them, and they yielded to the first few foothills of the Barrows.

"By Vulpus! I wish I could always run that fast," Vivi said, chest heaving.

"It's the only way to fly," Oscar wheezed, equally out of breath. He spied an ominous crag in the distance. "Though I normally wouldn't be in such a hurry to get here." While the full Jawbone range hid underneath a cloak of fog, the peak of Devilkin Mountain poked through, like the horn of some ravenous behemoth lying in wait for its next victim. The unnerving visage of the mountain fostered a debilitating feeling of dread in all who looked upon it, and these three were no exception.

Vivi gulped hard. "We've got to go *there?*"

"Yes, but first, we have to get through *this*," Annwyn said.

The flush of excitement and exhilaration first dampened by the nefarious mountain was now completely doused as the three friends surveyed the Barrows sprawled out in front of them, and they cringed at the sight. The ground was a cesspool, seeping with thick, black mud. Under a sulfurous haze, barren and contorted trees resembling charred remains stuck up out of the sludge, and bulbous, misshapen mounds of earth spread across the terrain like an infection. Horrid sucking and slurping sounds assailed their ears, along with the tormented wailing of the creatures doomed to inhabit this realm. A fetid stench filled the air and dared them to gag.

"This isn't exactly a picnic either," Annwyn noted dryly, "and you can barely see the path."

"Yeah, and it stinks like rotten eggs out here! Pew!" Vivi snipped.

"Well, at least there's no snow," Oscar said.

"Some silver lining."

Nonetheless, they girded themselves and went forward, the Barrows eagerly swallowing them. Oscar kept to the air, swooping from tree to tree and keeping an eye out for danger. Annwyn and Vivi trudged on, trying to keep their feet dry and out of the muck, but the trail was constantly seeping, slowing their progress to a crawl. Annwyn slipped, and the gurgling mire enveloped her left leg up to the thigh.

"Yuk! I'm all slimy!"

"You really stepped in it this time," Oscar said, snickering.

"Yeah, that's it, laugh. I'd like to see you come down here and walk for a little bit," Annwyn shot back. With no small effort, she pulled her leg free of the slop, which reluctantly let its morsel go. For good measure, she scooped a large handful of mud from her leg and flung it at the owl. Even with one eye, he was still agile enough to avoid being covered in the goop. Annwyn cleaned the rest of the cumbersome mud from her boot and pants, and they resumed their laggardly march.

Vivi stopped dodging mud puddles and looked all around, ears pointed to attention. "Hey, listen," she whispered.

"What's the matter?" Oscar asked.

"I don't hear anything, whatever was making all that noise when we got here has stopped. I don't like this at all…"

"Maybe whatever's out there is afraid of us," Oscar said, "maybe they're hiding."

"Maybe they're not," Annwyn cautioned, "let's quicken our pace."

They wisely heeded her advice and hastened down the sloppy path as best they could.

After struggling against the Barrows for an indeterminate amount of time, the trail brought them to the backside of the forbidding mountain where they found, with ease, the Witch's Hands: two old, blackened, sickly-looking trees standing side-by-side, contorted and gnarled as if they had been buried alive and vainly attempted to claw their way out of the stinking ground. The path ran between the profane trees, so they followed it for a short distance until they reached the base of Devilkin. At the end, they beheld an angular archway carved into the stone of the mountain. A large boulder sealed the entrance.

"This must be it," Oscar proclaimed. "That rock's gonna make it difficult to get in there. Think we can move it?"

"I don't know, it looks pretty heavy," Vivi said.

"Let's try." Oscar, Annwyn and Vivi each braced themselves against the boulder and pushed with all their might, until it felt like they would explode, but the enormous rock didn't budge one bit. They collapsed onto the ground, spent and breathing heavily. "I think we almost had it," Oscar cracked in between gulps of air.

"I'll let you finish it then," Vivi responded breathlessly.

The dots stopped dancing in front of Annwyn's eyes, and she sat up, resting on her knees. She surveyed the entrance and spied something peculiar on the top of the archway. "Hey, take a look. There's something there, strange markings."

"Where?" Oscar asked.

"Up there, look."

Oscar flew up and hovered in front of the crest of the archway, inspecting the scrawl. "Incredible…"

"What is it?"

"It's an inscription, and it's in Owlish."

"That's lucky," Vivi paused, "you can read it, can't you?"

"Sure."

"I didn't know owls wrote," Annwyn said.

"Yeah, we all used to a long time ago, before we learned how to pass on our instinctive memories, but since then, only the royal family and scholars keep the art alive. I had to study the language as part of my schooling to become king, but I found it kinda boring."

"How boring? Do you know what it says?" Annwyn asked.

"Let me see, I'm not exactly fluent, you know, but I can read it pretty well. Hmmm, it's in a weird dialect…." Oscar stared intently, silently cursing his past inability to pay attention to his kingly lessons without daydreaming. Then, in his mind, the symbols began fusing together, unlocking the secret knowledge they contained. "Aha! Here we go! It says: I race between earth and the heavens, and only I decide when my strength leavens. My presence can be felt everywhere, from highest mountaintop to deepest valley, if you dare. Yet whether sun or moon in the sky, I cannot been seen when I fly, and no shadow cast I."

"Are you reading it right? It doesn't make any sense," Annwyn said.

"I don't think it's supposed to. It sounds like a riddle," Vivi offered.

"Read it again, Oscar," Annwyn asked, and he obliged her. "What could it mean?" They all sat and mulled the question for a while, whispering contorted calculations to themselves under their breath. Finally, Annwyn snapped. "Oooh!!! We don't have time for this," she said in a huff, "I hate riddles!"

Vivi got up and began pacing, emitting a low growling: "Felt everywhere...mountaintops...no shadow...Oscar, does the riddle say anything else? Can it be read a different way?"

"If it can, I don't know how to do it. Drat! I know the answer's hiding right in front of us..."

"Just like everything else on this adventure," Annwyn said.

Oscar alighted next to her. "C'mon Annwyn, we'll figure it out. We got this far didn't we? We just need to concentrate. What flies under the sun and doesn't cast any shadows?" Too dispirited even to think, Annwyn let out a huge sigh that ruffled Oscar's feathers with the exhalation. "That's it! Annwyn, you're a genius!"

"Huh?"

Oscar gave her a peck on the cheek and flew to the boulder. He hovered before the ancient markings and said: "Wind."

As soon as the words left his beak, a great gale blew, and the friends had to take cover where they could find it to keep from being swept away. The zephyr whipped and twisted around the great bolder, wrenching it from where it sat to reveal a narrow entranceway into the caverns below. With the barrier cleared, the wind calmed to a gentle breeze and eventually dissipated with a hollow howl. A rumble of thunder convinced the three friends to enter the cave without delay, and they quickly left the foul Barrows behind them.

Lycurgus arrived at the Barrows shortly after the Owl King and the others ventured into Devilkin. Though he could not match the speed gifted them by that infernal nuisance living in Fir Hollow, he traveled on inter-dimensional pathways, known only to the creatures of shadow, which allowed him to circumvent most of the Meadmallow. He crept within sight of the Witch's Hands and just beyond them, he saw the massive stone resting beside the archway.

They must already be inside. He fought the immediate desire to slip inside and slay them, for he knew where they were headed and what horrors awaited them. He had not survived for so long by being rash, and though he had the means to dispatch the Demon of Devilkin Mountain, why not let them wake the slumbering beast? He would just pick through the scraps. Lycurgus slinked into the cave and became one with the darkness.

Creeping up over a hill overlooking the Witch's Hands, Dartmoor and Rowan saw Lycurgus follow Annwyn and Oscar into the cave. "Perfect timing," Dartmoor said, emitting a sinister laugh and eyes flashing with abject cruelty. He was growing more and more ghoulish by the hour; darkened purple veins latticed his waxy skin, and he continued to cough viscous blood, which left a putrescent crust on his lips. The stench of death clung to him.

"We goin' in then?" Rowan dared to ask, terrified at the thought of descending into the depths of Devilkin. He averted his eyes when Dartmoor glared at him. The specters, goblins and vampires which haunted Rowan's dreams were nothing compared to this rabid thing before him now. He winced when it spoke.

"No, you cretin, let them deal with the demon. Whoever comes out will die by my hand," he snarled, revealing sharpened, yellowing, bloodied teeth set in receding, graying gums. "For now, we wait." Dartmoor pulled his mount into the shadows of the Barrows. Rowan swallowed hard and followed, not sure what he feared most, the mountain or what was left of his friend.

Dandelion, Ash and Pooka still made their way on the Pebblestone Path, and with Fir Hollow in sight, the deer sped up from a sprint to a full gallop. They came to the end of the path and halted, pulling up in front of the dense copse; there was nothing unusual amid the melting but still deep snow, and no entrance was discernable in the tree line. The Flicker Brothers popped out to shed some light on the situation, but the limbs of tightly packed trees formed an impenetrable barrier to whatever was inside the hollow. The situation looked hopeless.

"Maybe we can squeeze between the trees," Ash proclaimed. "I've gotten through tighter spaces'n that before. What's a little sap?"

"No, Ash," Hart warned, "though they look like normal trees, the needles on those boughs are sharp as swords, and they would make quick work of you."

"No foolin'."

"Go ahead, Ash, give it a try," Dandelion giggled. Ash grumbled in response.

Grace noticed a disturbed snow bank with several partially filled-in footprints under some pine boughs on the edge of the copse. "Look, over here. These are definitely owl tracks, and these could be from a

Spriggin. Annwyn and Oscar were here not too long ago. Ah, it must be them; I'd recognize Vivi's paw-prints anywhere."

"Who's Vivi?" Dandelion asked.

"A fox who offered to guide Annwyn and Oscar here. She's a tad infamous for all her sneaking around Fir Hollow. She claims she discovered a secret entrance and even snuck in before, but it's hard to take a fox at her word. She must have found something, though, because their tracks end here. And look at this! Something must have swept aside the snow over here."

"I wanna see!" Dandelion hopped down off Grace's back and inspected the area. "This has gotta be it," she said. "Do you think we should just crawl through here? Oh right, the needles. Maybe we can tunnel in or something. Too bad I didn't bring the worms with me. Hart, any chance you know how to get past these trees?"

"No, Dandelion. We deer have never been inside the hollow before. All I can tell you is the entrance is hidden."

"Dang! Right back where we started." The exasperated Dandelion slumped in the snow. "Now what do we do?"

"Seems that's the only way in," Ash answered. "You guys wait here," he said to the deer, "we'll check it out. C'mon Pooka." He and Pooka dismounted their steeds, and all three Spriggins got down on their hands and knees and dug, trying to penetrate the snowy barricade, which bit their fingers each time they plunged their hands in.

Then, they heard a voice. "You could go that way, or you could pass easily through here." The trees separated, and the three Sprigs dove and rolled to avoid the moving limbs and their dagger-needles. Retreating to a safe distance, they observed a pathway leading into a lush grotto. A gust of toasty, delicious air enveloped them, the perfect antidote to the frigid conditions outside.

"Ohhh, that sure feels good," Dandelion delighted. "We couldn't ask for a warmer welcome." She took the lead, and the rest cautiously followed her through the parted trees. Once inside, a lightness entered their beings, tantalizing them with a taste of life from carefree days in happier times. Soon they came to a juncture of creeks offering multiple paths. They stopped and looked about. A faint rustling sounded from behind them.

"Be alert," Hart cautioned.

"Hello? Who's there?" Dandelion asked.

"It's me, the one you search for." They spun around a saw, poking up out of a dampened log, the Mushroom King.

"Are you, Ismene?"

"I am."

"Then do you know why we're here?"

"Ahh, indeed I do, indeed I do. I'm a fellow of many talents, young Spriggin. Is that not why you sought me?"

"I suppose," Dandelion said, nodding her head. "I'm Dandelion. This is Pooka and Ash, and—"

"No need for introductions, my young friend, you are all already known to me. I have some information you might find useful."

"Annwyn, Oscar. Where are they?" Pooka asked.

"I have sent them to Devilkin Mountain in search of the Moonstone. They have already made it into the caverns, but they are not alone. Dartmoor and Rowan are not far behind, but a greater evil stalks your friends. They are in great peril. You will need to quicken pace once you depart here if you are to help them. Luckily, this is a task most suited to you deer. You do know the way, don't you, Hart?"

"Yes, sir."

"Splendid! Now then, cross over Meadmallow, and follow the path through the Barrows to the backside of the mountain; there you will find a cave entrance that will lead you to your friends. Be warned, this will be no easy task. Your battle with the snakes was but a prelude to what is to come. Let's hope it is not too late."

"No time to waste," Pooka said, climbing onto Ama. The other Spriggins mounted their deer, and with newfound purpose, they bounded away, hooves pounding.

"Bye Ismene, it was really nice to meet you!" Dandelion called out, voice trailing off as they strode out of sight.

"Likewise, my dear, likewise."

Back inside the cave, Oscar, Annwyn and Vivi moved slowly, trying to decipher the path ahead of them. Annwyn had ignited the Emerald Flower and was guiding the way, but the footing was still unsure. It was dark, cold and slippery; water trickled down the cave walls, forming puddles underfoot. Outside of their footsteps, all that could be heard was the slight *plop* of water striking rock. They navigated through an array of spectacular, milky-white stalactites, stalagmites and pillars enhanced by the indirect jade lighting of Annwyn's ring. They marveled at the dazzling display of exquisite crystals exposed slowly over time by the relentless droplets of water. The light caught the angles of the crystals, causing them to sparkle and twinkle. It was as if piece of starry sky had wandered down from the heavens, ventured into the cave and been trapped underground.

The three companions continued on, too focused even to speak. Down here, one false move could mean death. Eventually, they came upon a natural limestone bridge that led them further and further into the depths of the cave. They had finally passed through the entrance zone and were now entering the twilight caverns, where no natural light was available. Only the slight cast of the ring reflected in the minerals allowed them to see where they were going, but the way was becoming more and more treacherous with each unsteady step. The closing darkness and the increased frequency and prominence of the spiky structures gave them the impression of being inside a giant predator's mouth as it closed on its prey. Then, they came to a deep, wide, elongated rift in the cave floor.

"How are we going to climb down this chasm without killing ourselves?" Vivi asked, dispirited.

"Don't worry, I'll fly around the gap and see if there's an easier way down," Oscar assured her.

He flew up into the endless void of the cavern. Unexpectedly, the heaviness in his heart grew lighter as he beat his wings, and he indulged in a taste of sweet distraction. He would find a way across the chasm in a moment; for now, he was content to give himself over to the freedom from earthly concerns only flight could offer. But, somewhere in the darkness, lost to his pleasure, he swooped too closely to a colony of resting bats, shocking them awake and overloading their senses with a haywire alarm; the skittish animals let go their grip on the ceiling and bolted away from the winged disruption, their screeches and squeaks echoing throughout the chamber. Oscar tried to dive back down to alert his friends, but he could not penetrate the blanket of bats below him.

Down at a lower altitude, Vivi perked her ears and tilted her head to the side: "What's that noise?" She peered into the inky blackness beyond the reach of the ring's glow. With her enhanced vision, she could make out a brown, hairy mass with flapping wings coming right at them. "Ahh! Duck!"

"Wha—!" Annwyn shouted, but she had no time for confusion, for Vivi jumped on her back, knocking her down and forcing her to lie prone on the ground. The little fox lay down on the Sprig, partially shielding her from the bats, and they covered their heads from the impending swarm. The discord produced by the bats' squeals was ear-splitting, amplified as it was by the cavern, and they could feel a million little brushes from wings and the whoosh of agitated air as the bats flew over them and into the ravine. Once the squeaking was barely audible, they knew they were in the clear. They picked themselves up, a little dirty and damp from hugging the cavern floor, and tried to regain what composure they could. "You okay, Vivi?"

"Sure, I'm lucky I didn't get bitten. Bats are so cranky when they're disturbed. How 'bout you?"

"No bites here, just a little smudgy." Annwyn titled her head up toward the ceiling. "Thanks for the company, Oscar!" she called up to him. "Do you think you could manage to make this experience any more unpleasant?" She saw the winged troublemaker swoop down just low enough to flash a grin not wholly appreciated by his friends.

"You're welcome. Just trying to keep your own your toes, or I guess, in this case, your stomachs," Oscar giggled as he flew out of sight again.

"I guess he's cheered up."

"Owl King or no, he just earned himself a nip," Vivi huffed. She returned to investigating, sniffing and poking about for a bit when she noticed an old, dilapidated staircase set back into the cavern walls. "Hey, I've found something."

"What is it?" Annwyn asked.

"A way to the bottom, maybe?"

Annwyn walked cautiously over to Vivi and looked at the ramshackle excuse for a stairway. "You want to walk down those?"

"It's better than falling down them."

"I guess you're right. But who put this stairway here? Where does it lead?"

"Your guess is as good as mine, Annwyn."

"I suppose. Well, let's collect our friend. Oscar, where are you?" Annwyn yelled, her voice bouncing off the walls and repeating the question a hundred times. Suddenly, he swooped down out of nowhere, taking them aback and making them scream in a panic. "AHHH!!! Oscar! Don't ever do that!" Annwyn panted, grasping her chest.

Vivi let out a little growl at her tormentor—first the bats, now this. Under ordinary circumstances, this owl would have already earned himself a bite. "Grrrr, it must be tough work pulling double duty as the king and the jester!"

"Sorry, I just wanted to let you know I didn't find anything."

"Well, Vivi found something," Annwyn replied, still trying to recover from the fright.

"Mmm, looks dangerous," Oscar said, surveying the rickety stairwell. "Annwyn, you go first."

"My hero." She held the ring up for light and tested the first step. It creaked and wobbled even though she hadn't put that much weight on it, and she nearly lost her footing.

"Seems sturdy enough," Oscar said, slapping Annwyn on the back with his wing.

"I should make you carry me, you know." Annwyn shrugged off Oscar's wing. "Let's go, Vivi."

The little fox followed Annwyn down the stairs while Oscar hovered behind them. The light from the Emerald Flower waned even more, and the going was slow. Steadily, they made their way down and once at the bottom, the Emerald Flower sparked back to life and hummed with an even greater intensity than before, illuminating the entire cavern. It revealed a vast, still lake, with only a thin stretch of gray shoreline between them and the icy waters.

"Oh, great, how're we supposed to get across this?" Vivi howled.

"Well, I can fly across, maybe. See what's on the other side," Oscar offered.

"Do you think you can make this flight a little less eventful than the last one, ace?" Vivi growled. "I'm not sure how much guano I need in my fur today, but I think I'm good."

"Sorry, I don't make promises I can't keep," he said with a wink. "Don't worry, I'll be back in a jiff."

"It's not you I'm worried about," Annwyn spoke, her voice discordant with anxiety and dampening the jovial atmosphere. "Oscar, don't go."

The Owl King sensed something in Annwyn's voice, and it froze him in his tracks. "Yeah, I think you're right."

A feeling of dread crept over the three, like they were being hunted, and with it, the cavern grew still, too still even for a place nestled so far in the bowels of the earth. The steady drips of water that bounced through the caverns on the way down had stopped. The air turned stale and sour, and all they could hear was the beating of their own hearts. There was something out there. The terrible silence was broken when, from somewhere in the darkness, they heard a bubbling sound; the water within the purview of the Emerald Flower began to ripple, and then, off in the distance, they noticed a dim light coming from beneath the surface.

Vivi ventured forward to the edge of the shore. "What is that?"

"I don't know, but whatever it is, it can't be good," Oscar said warily. The light grew stronger and revealed the outline of a massive form underwater, making its way from the depths directly toward them. "Here it comes!"

The three of them fell back and took cover behind some stalagmites just as the Demon of Devilkin Mountain burst forth from the lake in an explosion of spray. It let out a deafening roar, exposing rows and rows of jagged teeth set in its huge, gaping mouth. It had hateful, yellow eyes and was covered with hundreds of barbed spikes. The demon stood upright and strode forward, its tail slapping the water in its wake. Its slimy, black hide glistened except for its belly, which was pale and luminous.

"Look out!" Oscar yelled. Just as the demon swung at them with a ropy arm, Oscar launched into the air, and Vivi tucked tail and ran while Annwyn rolled to avoid being crushed. The demon's claws created sparks when it struck the stalagmites, shattering them into a million pieces. The sheer force of the blow caused Annwyn to lose her balance. She landed on her stomach, knocking the wind out of her and leaving her exposed for a moment. The beast let out a squeal of delight and moved toward her. It raised its arm for another strike when Oscar flew into its face, using his talons to tear at its eyes.

"Leave her alone!" he yelled. The agitated monster swatted at him, and Oscar flew out over the lake, drawing the demon away from his friends.

Vivi rushed over to the downed Spriggin. "Annwyn, Annwyn, are you okay?"

Annwyn turned over and coughed. "Uh, yeah." She saw Oscar battling the demon offshore and noticed its glowing belly. "Vivi, look, that's got to be the Moonstone in there! We've got to get it out!"

"How are we gonna do that?" Vivi cried. "There's only one way down there, and that's by being that thing's dinner!"

"That's it!"

"Whatever you guys are planning, make sure you do it quick!" Oscar yelled, dodging the beast's snapping mouth.

He darted and twirled with great skill, but the beast was not easily deterred. He knew that at any moment, the demon's speed would catch up with him, and he would be shredded by those horrid teeth. Only Oscar's superior ears kept him from being a meal for the demon, since he could hear the water split the moment before the nightmarish creature burst forth from the depths. The loss of his eye would have normally put him at a terrible disadvantage, but since it was pitch black where he was, save for the light the monster produced, two eyes wouldn't have done much more to keep him safe than one. Besides, how often had he hunted for his supper in total darkness? More times than he could remember. But this was no comfort, for in that scenario, he was the terror that struck out of the darkness, not the victim.

The beast kept diving under the water and breaching, lunging at the elusive feathery snack, and with each empty mouthful, its rage grew. Unexpectedly, the demon threw itself out of the water more quickly than Oscar could anticipate and grabbed hold of his tail feathers with its teeth. The small owl knew terror, and he found himself pressed up against the demon's face, quickly headed for an icy, watery grave. He dug his claws into the monster's lower jaw and strained with all his might. He pulled himself free of the beast a split second before it dove back under the water, a few striped feathers sticking out from its closed mouth. The shaken owl steadied himself and flew a little higher than he had before. Panic welled up inside him since the loss of those feathers meant the loss of maneuverability, and his flying was unsteady at best. Any longer in the air and he wouldn't have to worry about a few missing tail feathers since he would be no match for the demon in this state. He looked back at his diminished plumage.

"AHH! Those feathers take forever to grow back! ANNWYNN! HURRY!!!"

"Hold on, Oscar!" Annwyn shouted. She hunkered down with the little fox. "Vivi, when I tell you, do you think you can get on that thing's tail and give it a good bite?"

Vivi's eyes bulged: "You want me to do *WHAT?*"

"Trust me, this is the only way. I know you can do this!"

"Alright, I'm in."

"Good, now just sit tight. Oscar! Oscar, lead him over here, close to shore!" Annwyn bellowed.

"It's about time you took your turn!" Oscar darted out of the demon's reach and flew back to shore. The demon immediately dove and followed him, creating a huge swell of water. Oscar looked back and saw the beast gaining on him. "He's coming!"

Annwyn stood. She thrust her right fist forward, and the emerald ring vibrated as it pulsed with a tremendous power. She grabbed her wrist with her left hand to brace against the growing energy. Oscar swooped over Annwyn's head, and just behind him, the demon exploded out of the water and came for her.

She gritted her teeth, and the Emerald Flower became as bright as the sun, blinding the demon and causing it to thrash and writhe in agony. "Vivi, go!"

The little fox zipped to the water and leapt in. She paddled furiously, and after a few close calls with the monster's flailing tail, she climbed onto the slippery appendage and got her footing by anchoring herself with her claws.

"Oscar, when the demon opens up, fly in there and get the Moonstone!" Annwyn shouted.

"ARE YOU CRAZY?!"

"No, but you are! Vivi, now!" At that, Vivi dug her claws the rest of the way in, reared back, and bit down as hard as she could through the beast's oily hide. She wanted to gag from the malignant taste in her mouth, but through sheer force of will hung on; her friends' lives depended on her. The demon roared in pain and its mouth flew wide open. "Go, Oscar!"

The Owl King took off and jetted up into the air. He reached the apex of his climb and changed trajectory: straight for the demon's gaping maw. He tucked his wings and dive-bombed into the beast's gullet. The shock from this unexpected attack caused the demon to buck, and Vivi was thrown clear from its tail; she slammed into a low-hanging stalactite and lay limp on the shore. Annwyn held fast to the still blazing ring. She could see Oscar's dark shape blotting out the glow from inside the demon's belly as it struggled in the water, continuously breaching in hopes of forcing the owl to stop tearing into its stomach with his claws. Suddenly, it turned toward the shore and lurched for Annwyn, opening its mouth to devour the interloper with the ring and its painful light. Annwyn had never seen anything so horrible in all her life; it was as if she was staring into an abyss filled with all the pain, hatred and evil in the world.

Oscar shot out of that abyss with the Moonstone firmly in his talons. He landed, a little dazed and a lot gooey, on his back a few feet from Annwyn. "I got it, Annwyn! I got it!" He held the glowing white stone out.

Annwyn fired up the Emerald Flower again, this time so brightly she had to squeeze her eyes closed, and the afterimage of the demon's mouth burned itself into her mind. Bolts of energy shot out of the ring and stunned the demon, stopping it suddenly like it had run into the cavern wall behind her; it held still for a moment, its jaws silently opening and closing before sliding back into the water to nurse its wounds. The wake from the monster's charge reached the shore and soaked Annwyn. She dared to look over at her friend.

"Oscar!" Annwyn dropped her arm and ran to her friend, causing the blazing light from the ring to stop. She knelt down and hugged him. The demon regained its senses, and it shrieked with rage. It lifted its head, and it fixed its blazing, yellow eyes on them and charged.

"Oh no! It's still coming!" Oscar screamed.

Annwyn turned around and prepared herself for oblivion. Using the ring to repel the beast had drained her, and she knew she did not have the strength to stop it again. If she was to die, at least she would be with her friend. She lurched forward to cover Oscar from the brunt of the demon's wrath when the most amazing thing happened. The Emerald Flower touched the Moonstone in Oscar's outstretched foot, and it shot forth a blazing beam of energy, striking the foul creature in the face. The demon's flesh melted away into a thick sludge, which hissed and dissipated upon hitting the water. Annwyn and Oscar had to shield their eyes from the intensity of the light. Soon the magnetic pull between the ring and stone ceased, and they separated, the beam of energy breaking up and fizzling out. Annwyn and Oscar fell back onto the shore, their bodies alternately tingling and numb.

Oscar sat up, and it was a moment before his eye adjusted to the dark. Steam rose from the surface of the lake where the demon met its demise. He spun his head around and was relieved to see Annwyn, alive but dazed, on her knees and struggling to steady herself on rubber arms. He spun his head around the other way to survey his surroundings when he saw the most curious thing. "Hey Annwyn, take a look."

"What is it?" She finally righted herself and sat back on the shore. She held her ring up so she could see.

There, in front of them, was a tiny green frog.

"*Ribbit*, thank you for releasing me from the curse," he croaked.

Annwyn could scarcely believe her eyes. "Who are you? Where did you come from?"

"You're the guardian, aren't you?" Oscar asked.

"Aye, I'm called Fergus, and I have suffered for many years, trapped inside that abomination and this dank pit. I can't even begin to describe how, *ribbit,* horrible it has been. I want to breathe fresh air again, feel the sun on my skin and the cool kiss of a stream. If you would, please, take me with you. I know a secret way to the surface, *ribbit.*"

"Consider it done, as long as you don't try to eat us again," Oscar said and rolled onto his stomach, using his wings to get to his feet. "Where's Vivi?"

"Oh, no! Vivi!" Annwyn ran over to the fox who was still lying lifeless on the shore. "Vivi, please wake up!" The tail twitched. "Oh, you're alive!"

"Mmmm, my aching head," Vivi whimpered. She stood on shaky legs and nearly fell over when she shook out her fur, sending out a spray of frigid droplets. "That's better."

"Think you can make it out of here?" Oscar asked.

"Sure, I'm none the worse for wear," she said, attempting a laugh that turned into a cough. "Ugh, talk about an aftertaste..." She spit and hacked, trying to rid herself of the rancid flavor in her mouth from the demon's flesh. She trotted down to the water's edge and began lapping at the water, not realizing she was drinking from the same spot where the monster's flesh had melted. She got only a half of a mouthful down when she spit it out with a loud "BLECHH!"

"Oh yeah, Vivi, don't drink the water," Oscar kidded.

The cross fox eyed him. She had suffered many indignities this day, and this was the last. "I know what'll get rid of this taste!" She dropped down like she was hunting voles back at the hollow and leaped at the Owl King.

Unaware of the grudge Vivi was nursing, Oscar wasn't ready for the sudden assault and feebly attempted to take off. But Vivi wouldn't be denied, and she caught hold of his already depleted tail feathers and pinched them together with her teeth. She pinned the Owl King down and peppered him with little nips, not enough to hurt, but enough to get her point across. Oscar kicked free and clumsily flew out of the range of the frenetic Vivi.

"OW!!! That hurts!"

"Oh, it does not, you big baby!" Vivi taunted. The two of them eyed each other for another moment before Oscar landed back on the shore.

Then, the little fox noticed the frog next to Annwyn. "Hey, who's this?"

"I'm Fergus. I was bound inside the demon until you freed me. I'm here to help."

"Good, you can make up for my splitting headache."

"I'm sorry about that. I had no control over my actions…"

"Don't worry, Fergus, you don't need to apologize. Now, where's this secret passage of yours?" Annwyn inquired.

"*Ribbit*, follow me." The frog hopped off into the recesses of the cave. Annwyn put the Moonstone in the pouch with her flute, and they followed him into the shadows.

Another shadow followed them.

Ama and Pooka tore across the grasslands with the others following their lead. The sky was no longer a darkened mass, and though the sun came out, making it lighter, it still was not clear since angry thunderheads percolated and spread across the heavens. The snow had melted away significantly since they left Fir Hollow, so it was barely to their ankles in the mounds that remained, and millions of stalks of grass eagerly sliced through the freezing blanket and availed themselves to the open air. The haze burned off a bit under the heat, so that the mountains, especially Devilkin, were faintly visible on the horizon.

The sight of the giant mountain filled Pooka with anxiety. "How much longer before we reach the Barrows?" he shouted.

"Up ahead, you can see the smog from here!" Ama replied. They saw the foggy expanse of the Barrows as they crested a small hill at the border of the Meadmallow. A huge clap of thunder shook the sky and the earth, bringing the deer to a halt.

"What was that?" Ash asked incredulously.

"I don't know, but it doesn't sound good," Hart replied.

A few lesser rumbles rolled across the sky and with them, the dark clouds thickened and took on a fiery appearance, billowing with thick, acrid vapors from within. "I've never seen a sky like that before," Dandelion said, wide-eyed.

"No one has," Ama added.

Hart snorted and stomped a hoof: "If what Ismene said is true, then we have little time."

Pooka furrowed his brow: "Whatever it is, we need to find Annwyn and Oscar before it gets worse! Let's go!"

Fergus was the first out of the cave opening hidden by scraggly and nearly barren bushes on the side of the mountain. The others emerged behind him to find themselves at a dizzying altitude well above the cloud line; they witnessed a breathtakingly gorgeous panoramic view of all the Known Realms, from the Dryder Swamps and Everdrop Falls all the way to Glassgrain Desert and Summerwind Coast. The other peaks of the Jawbone Mountains were visible this high up, and it was obvious how they got their name. The natural beauty of the landscape stood in drastic contrast to the way down the mountain: a narrow, steep, craggy path wending downward into a thick blanket of yellowish and foul-smelling nebula. What was beyond that was anyone's guess.

"I'm glad I can fly," Oscar said, looking down at the precarious pass.

Annwyn poked him. "Rub it in, why don't ya? Is it safe, Fergus?"

"*Ribbit*, I don't know. I've only been this way once, and that was on the way in. We'll just have to find out."

He turned and began down the trail. Annwyn and Vivi followed, taking care to keep low to maintain their footing, especially through the dense mists, where there was almost no visibility, even with the light Annwyn generated from the Emerald Flower. Oscar glided down, perching on pinnacles where he found them and giving scouting reports for any upcoming trouble-spots. Eventually, Annwyn, Vivi and Fergus, who opted to travel on the fox's back, descended all the way down the side of Devilkin and into the crevasse that would lead them to the Barrows and beyond.

Vivi, scouting ahead of Annwyn, lifted her snout to the wind and perked her ears. "Something is out there. I can smell it." They all stopped.

"If you can smell it out here, it must be bad," Annwyn said.

Fergus crawled up to Vivi's ear: "What is it?" She didn't answer; she was trying desperately to place the alarming scent, but this was unlike anything she'd ever encountered before. Oscar tilted his head to listen while Annwyn and Fergus looked all around. Now they all could sense it, the creeping dread of being hunted. They were exposed where they were in the middle of the path; so far down into the fissure, there was only one way out. Something tumbled down the rock face, and its clatter echoed throughout the canyon. The Emerald Flower flared in warning.

"Let's get out of here," Vivi whispered.

Before Annwyn could take a step, Lycurgus dropped down behind her and pinned her to the ground. He reared up to strike when Vivi and Fergus simultaneously pounced on him. Fergus covered an eye, and Vivi sunk her teeth deep into the soft flesh connecting the spider's head and body. Lycurgus hissed in pain and flung his assailants from his back, knocking them unconscious. The giant spider exposed his fangs and turned on the dazed Spriggin.

"NO!" Oscar swooped down with outstretched talons, and sunk them deep into Lycurgus's large eye. The owl pulled with all his might, and flew back into the air in a spray of gore, the eye in his claws. The spider lurched in pain and abandoned the Spriggin for the moment. Oscar dropped his bloody prize and maneuvered over Lycurgus's awaiting bite, tearing into his opponent's abdomen and causing blood to stream from the wound. A few more passes from the owl left Lycurgus soaked in his own juices.

But Lycurgus's skill caught up with Oscar, and he leapt with lightning speed, bringing down the Owl King in mid-air. They slammed into the ground, Oscar face down. Lycurgus pressed down on the owl with all his strength, trying to soften him up for the kill. Oscar struggled under the great weight, and managed to turn his head completely around, until he faced the seeping wound inflicted by Vivi. Straining until it felt like his spine would snap, he thrust his beak forward and bit through the tender flesh, whipping his head and tearing Lycurgus in half. Oscar found himself trapped under the headless abdomen, which spewed foul gunk all over him. The front half of the giant spider flailed for a moment before landing on its back, its legs shuddering and finally shriveling up. The beast collapsed and moved no more. Oscar worked his head free.

"Annwyn, are you okay? Uhh, I can't move my wing."

"Hold on, Oscar." Annwyn groggily got to her feet and stumbled over to her friend.

"He's fine where he is!"

Annwyn spun around, and there were Dartmoor and Rowan atop their wolf spiders. "You have something that belongs to me, Annwyn." The cadaverous Dartmoor jumped down from his mount and approached the top half of Lycurgus. "How fitting." He spit on the spider's corpse and tore loose one of the giant fangs. Annwyn collapsed with fear and revulsion as he approached her with the weapon. She could do nothing but stare at his demonic visage. "You should never have crossed me, foolish girl! Now, for what's mine," he said, raising the venomous dagger over his head.

"Dartmoor, NO!" Oscar roared.

The depraved Spriggin plunged the fang into Annwyn's shoulder. She let out a slight gasp and wilted, and the last sparks of light from within the Emerald Flower crackled and died. Dartmoor wheezed with pleasure and pulled the shiv free. He cut the pouch from her waist, reached in, and pulled out the Moonstone, its opalescent shimmer fading slightly in his grasp. Tossing the pouch aside, he beheld his spoil and raised it over his head.

"It's mine! And soon I will wield the ultimate power!" The sky crackled with thunder.

"You'll pay for this, Dartmoor! You'll pay with your life!"

Dartmoor coughed and blood trickled from the corner of his mouth. "Shut up! I think I'll leave you here to rot and watch your precious Annwyn die." He spit on the owl's face and mounted his spider. "Back to the village."

Dartmoor and Rowan quickly scuttled out of sight, leaving Oscar's tormented screams to fill the crevasse.

The deer had just broken into the Barrows when they heard the Owl King's cries off to their right.

"Let's go!" Pooka shouted, and the group bounded toward the source. They came upon the craggy trailhead and dove into the canyon where they soon discovered the gruesome remains of Lycurgus surrounded by the lifeless forms of Annwyn, Vivi and Fergus. "ANNWYN!" Pooka cried and jumped down from a still-moving Ama. He rolled when he hit the ground and gathered her up, cradling her to his chest. "Annwyn! She's hurt! Dandelion, I need your medicine! Hurry!"

Grace skidded to a halt next to Pooka and Dandelion dismounted, removing her pack and rifling through it to find her healing herbs. She produced the pouch and rapidly prepared and applied a field dressing to Annwyn's wound. Pooka was intently monitoring the ministrations when he heard a strained, desperate voice call out.

"Help! It's me, Oscar! Help, I'm trapped!" Under a pile of gore in the gulley, they spied the Owl King entombed under the oozing carcass of the once-great Lycurgus.

"Hold still, Oscar!" Ash shouted. Hart lowered his antlers, pierced the abdomen, and flung it aside, freeing the Owl King, who shook off the slimy remains of his adversary from his feathers.

"We need to get back to Willow Hills! Dartmoor's on his way there now with the Moonstone!"

"Oh no," Dandelion whimpered over her rapidly deteriorating friend, "my herbs aren't working! She's dying!"

"She's not finished yet, Dandelion. The ring she's wearing reacts with the Moonstone. If we can get it back, we can save her!" Oscar trilled.

"Collect the others, we need to move!" Pooka ordered. He lifted Annwyn onto Ama's back and mounted the deer. Ash jumped down, picked up Vivi and carried her over his shoulder. He scooped up Fergus and gave him to Dandelion, who put the little frog in her pocket. Ash got back on Hart and secured the fox in front of him.

Oscar took to the air. "This way!" he shouted, and the group bolted off under a menacing and fiery sky.

CHAPTER 10

The Maelstrom

Back in the throne room under Glenna's watchful stare, Cornish contacted their son again. *Dartmoor, what do you have to report?* He listened intently and then grinned: *Well done, my boy. I expect you shortly.* Cornish's eyes rolled back from inside his skull. He was now wearing the Owl King's crown in hopes that its inherent, latent powers would grant him the ability to tame the primordial, evil leviathan he had unleashed in the Maelstrom. Nothing worked. The crown had no discernable effect on the binding bewitchments, incantations and charms he conjured, and the archaic tome he used for spellcasting proved no more effective than reading from a student primer. Cornish had endured repeated beatings from Glenna since his last failed conjuration, and he cursed her masterful manipulation of magic, which kept him in thrall of her. It did not help matters that just the sight of the crown on her ineffectual underling's head caused Glenna to unleash her fears upon him. Cornish dared to meet his wife's eyes with the look of a whipped dog.

"Well?"

"He has the Moonstone," he mewled, "the Owl King and Annwyn Bluebell are taken care of. Lycurgus is dead, however."

"Bah, no matter, there's more where that came from," she said, waving her hand dismissively, causing Cornish to tremble. "When will our son arrive?"

He dithered under her intense gaze, and slunk back into his throne, bracing for another strike. "He will be here within hours. And when he does arrive, I will use the Moonstone to regain mastery of the Maelstrom. So, my love, we have no reason to fear."

"*I* have no reason to fear, you mean. You had better pray this works, *my love*," she bared her teeth, and Cornish flinched. He gripped the arms of his throne with sweaty palms, and his head snapped back, lacerated by the harpy's claws. "Get thee down to the dungeon and await our son. I can't stand to have you in my sight any further!" The shredded Spriggin acquiesced and left to terrorize his prisoners. Outside, a barrage of thunder battered the skies, causing the entire palace to quiver, as if cowering at what the storm brought with it.

The deer blazed back down the grasslands, for the snow had melted, and within an hour, they could make out the northern edge of

Anglia Forest on the horizon. The molten sky grew thick with menacing clouds, which catapulted arcs of flame across the atmosphere, igniting the air around them in a deluge of flares. The concomitant increase in temperature kicked up powerful winds, forming twisters that stabbed into the grasslands, leaving it pocked and barren where they touched down. The thunder roared ever louder, its ardor threatening to split the earth apart. Off in the distant sky, somewhere over the deep forest, a whirling dervish of a funnel cloud whirred violently until its thrashing tore open the sky, revealing a blackened void beyond. The aperture acted like a magnet, drawing the flaming firmament toward it and gaining strength with each of the angry clouds it swallowed. Vivi and Fergus had long since woken up to the chaos, she perched on Hart's back with Ash, while the frog rode in the relative comfort of Dandelion's front pocket, where the lightning bugs also huddled. As the group moved on, deer who had been on patrol rejoined the herd, swelling its ranks the further down the veldt it galloped. All the while Oscar soared overhead, using his wings to string the updrafts of wind together into an uninterrupted, effortless flight.

But Pooka saw none of this. All that mattered to him was Annwyn, and she had not moved once since he'd secured her on Ama's back. She had grown cold, and her skin turned deathly pale. Her essence waned, and Pooka felt her slipping away. Continuing to hold her tight, he fought to keep his emotions in check, the blistering skies no match for the fervid animus burning within him.

"Hey, I see something up ahead," Oscar called out, "is that—it's Dartmoor!"

Pooka snapped to attention, and his eyes narrowed when he spied Dartmoor and Rowan gliding on their striding spiders toward the edge of the forest. Dartmoor had infused the spider-steeds with a charm of windwalking to grant them incredible speed, but they could not outpace the deer forever. Pooka spurred Ama forward, and she responded with astonishing acceleration.

"Pull alongside Dartmoor!"

"Hold on!"

She dropped her head and charged even harder. She halved the distance to the spiders when a colossal thunderclap cracked the sky open, and a fiery meteor hurled toward the plains. It impacted and exploded, showering flaming debris in every direction and causing Ama to jump, dodge and swerve out of the way of the deadly detritus. More and more blistering projectiles hammered down from the sky, forcing the group to split apart to avoid being instantly incinerated. Hart took point and the herd fell in behind him.

"Everybody, on my mark, break formation! Get to the woods and take cover; we'll meet up at the village! Break formation…NOW!"

At this command, Grace sprinted off to the left; the buck and his passengers veered to the right; the rest of the deer disbanded, scattering across the grassland and improvising their paths, deftly feinting and juking past the devastating meteorites. Ignoring the raining missiles, Pooka and Ama continued their desperate pursuit of Dartmoor, attempting to retake the scoundrel among the destruction.

Meanwhile, Oscar's instinctual ability to fly took over, and he evaded the meteors with uncanny prowess. He climbed a thermal draft and rode it to its apex, shifting his direction as his inertia caught up with him so that he targeted Dartmoor. Oscar tucked his wings, leaned forward and plummeted, the world blurring on the descent. Almost indistinguishable from the other fiery shafts filling the sky, the enraged owl closed in on his foe.

"This is for my father!" He exposed his talons and strafed Dartmoor, laying open the decaying skin of his face in spurts of black blood and nearly tossing him from his spider. Oscar looped around for another pass.

"Ahh! Blackthorn, do something!"

"Hey flyboy, take this!" Sitting sidesaddle on his spider, Rowan produced his slingshot and loosed a buckeye at the Owl King. Oscar cut hard to the right, but he misjudged the pellet's trajectory since it crossed his blind spot, and it grazed the side of his head, taking a few feathers with it, knocking him off balance and forcing him to roll to regain control. "Ha! Ha! That got 'im!" Oscar steadied himself quickly, but Rowan and Dartmoor ably tripled the distance between the owl and them by the time he hit stride again.

The sky was brimstone now, and the red-hot rock shellacked the earth in an even greater combustive bombardment than before. Sizzling shrapnel whizzing past his face, Pooka gained on his nemesis and was about to grasp hold of his tattered robe when Dartmoor pulled on his spider's reins. In one fluid motion, it spun around and began running backwards without breaking stride while several orbs scurried onto its abdomen, secured themselves, and released hundreds of silk strands which bound together, catching the gusting wind and pulling Dartmoor and his arachnid transporter straight up into the air. Now facing Pooka, Dartmoor waved mockingly at the anguished Spriggin as his spider landed on top of the canopy of the trees, spun forward again, and kept running.

Rowan's steed loosed its own silken parachute and followed Dartmoor up top. "Better luck next time!"

"We're not done yet, Pooka!" Ama shouted. "I've yet to meet the spider that can outrun me!" She evaded an igneous bolt and plunged into the forest, dodging the trees with such fluidity that they lost no speed. Pooka looked over to his right to see Hart and Ash break through the tree line. A loud rustle to his left let him know Grace and Dandelion had survived Meadmallow, too. Several other fortunate deer entered the wood, and the herd regrouped and plowed ahead. Though the forest provided greater cover than the grassland, the meteors easily broke through the canopy, splintering the trees in their path and setting the surrounding ones ablaze like tinder. The fire spread rapidly, threatening to engulf all of Anglia in an inferno.

"Look, there they are!" Dandelion shouted, pointing to the treetops; there they saw the undersides of the spiders above them. A shadow darted through the sky and struck one of the riders like an arrow; a bloodied Rowan crashed through the canopy and broke several limbs on his way down to the ground, landing in a particularly thick patch of briars and vanishing from sight. The shadow zipped across the sky again, and the spider disappeared for a brief moment before its entrails splattered on the understory.

"You're next, Nettle!" Oscar yelled. He closed in, but before he could strike, a massive fireball broke through the trees right behind Dartmoor and exploded in a giant conflagration. Oscar barely escaped being obliterated, and the deer hardly had enough time to pull up and avoid being vaporized. Dartmoor scurried out of sight. "You guys alright down there?"

"We're fine," Pooka hollered back. "Oscar, keep track of him, and we'll meet you back at Willow Hills!"

"Got it. See you there!"

"I know another way," Hart said. "Follow me."

They took off toward the village.

Llangollen had a few more strands left to sever to be free of his cell when an earthquake struck, shaking the dungeon violently and knocking everyone down. The webbed cells stretched and snapped some, but they did not break. Quakes were not common in these parts, and the shock of it overloaded the sentries' senses; they quit the chamber as quickly as their rustling limbs would carry them. Once it passed, the prisoners found themselves unattended, though the tremor's shockwave flung them against the tacky webbing lining their cells, and they struggled to get free.

While they pulled and yanked against their restraints, Llangollen shouted, "Where'd that come from?"

"Don't know," Abe said. "Is anyone hurt?"

They all vouched for their hardiness one-by-one, and wrested themselves free. The guards were not coming back, leaving the exit unguarded, and the initial hole Llangollen cut into his cell wall had not resealed itself during the quake. This was their chance. "Oden, can you bite through the wrapping on your feet?" he called out.

"We'll make short work of those webs!"

Llangollen hugged his wife and kissed her. "Alright sweetie, keep an eye out for the guards."

"Be careful."

"Of course, am I ever anything but? Okay folks! As soon as you get out, make a break for the surface."

Llangollen again stooped down behind the cover Gwilyn provided, and set to work shredding the cell wall with the proboscis. The ground trembled again, and a horrid, bloodcurdling shriek from within Queen Erebus's chamber pierced their ears and sent the Sprigs to their knees as the owls clacked their beaks in agony. Perry whimpered and clung to his mother.

When the pain in his head subsided, Oden sliced through the last of the webbing binding his feet. He took a second to stretch his toes out before grabbing hold of the wall and shearing it open with his talons. He rushed out into the chamber and was soon joined by Sadé, Oakley and Ludwig. They fluttered over to the Spriggins' cells.

"Stand back, we'll get you out of there!" The Sprigs hunkered down and the owls sliced the webbing like rice paper. "Alright, let's go!"

"Oh no! Look behind you!" Perry cried out. The owls turned their heads and there, in the doorway, were Cornish and the guards.

Dartmoor spurred his spider faster and faster across the treetops. The bewitched arachnid's augmented reflexes kept them safe enough from the fireballs, but no amount of sorcery would deny Oscar. He beat his wings in concert with the torrents of wind, using their power to draw within striking distance. He spread his talons in anticipation, and at the same moment he swiped at Dartmoor, the cur and his spider slid below the canopy, leaving Oscar grasping at twigs and leaves. The spider jumped from limb to limb, descending to the forest floor with incredible speed and fluidity. It hit the ground running with the deer in hot pursuit.

"There he is!" Pooka shouted. They chased Dartmoor, but he made full use of the cover provided by the fire raining down, always managing to force the deer into the path of an explosion, and they could not gain the last bit of ground to overtake him. Soon the forest thinned out and gave way to the clearing leading to Willow Hills. The web barrier around the village had been struck by multiple meteors and was now ablaze, with whole sections of it completely burned away. If possible, Dartmoor's mount gained more momentum once the village was in sight. Oscar sliced through the canopy and weaved past the trees to drop down behind his nemesis. They continued their chase into the village, but beheld a terrible sight.

"Oh no!" Dandelion wailed.

Conflagrant meteors had struck all over Willow Hills, causing many houses and trees to catch fire while some were simply pulverized from the impacts. Screaming Spriggins fleeing from their destroyed homes filled the streets, looking for shelter. The fearsome barrage forced the spiders patrolling the village to abandon their posts and take cover, so some of the herd broke off to collect up wayward Sprigs and get them to safety. The others dodged the teeming masses in their pursuit of Dartmoor, who guided his mount onto the rooftops and through all the chaos before reaching the web palace, his hunters not far behind.

"What's this abomination?" Ash yelled.

"I don't know, but that's where we're going!" Oscar shouted. He sped forward and was nearing Dartmoor when the spider jumped an impossible distance, landed on the side of the palace, and scurried up a spire, latching onto a veranda and vanishing inside. Orbs immediately emerged from the wall and sealed closed the way behind him. Oscar overshot his mark and had to turn back around to meet the others. They pulled up in front of the imposing barricade.

"We've got to get in there," Pooka gritted his teeth. "I won't let him escape!"

"I'm going in!" Oscar exclaimed. But the second he lifted off, the ornate palace doors swung open and a horde of warrior spiders poured out, climbing over the outer wall and encircling them. The meteors did not deter these spiders; their only aim was to protect their queen. The deer closed ranks, their backs to each other.

"On my signal, follow me," Hart spoke quietly. He snorted and tossed his head, his deadly antlers causing the spiders closest to them to retreat.

"Hart, let's not make any rash decisions," Ash's voice quivered, "remember you got me and a fox back here."

"No, wait," Pooka said, "I know what to do." He loosened his grip on Annwyn and secured her against Ama, jumped down and removed his pack, hundreds of tiny, beady eyes focusing on every move he made. He slowly pulled out his drum, and nestling it in the crook of his left arm, he raised his right hand over his head and held it there, poised to strike. "You all know what this does, don't you?"

"Pooka, what're you doing?" Oscar nervously hooted.

"Trust me," he answered, hand hovering over the drum.

Inside the Fairy Circle, however, the owls could not see what was happening; they could only hear the whizzing of the projectiles and feel the seismic quakes with each impact. Unfortunately, none of the meteors struck the webbing of the circle, leaving the owls trapped inside. The spiders, their vigilance replaced by fear, skittered randomly around the amphitheater, confused and terrified by the vibrations. Even Ulric could not maintain his discipline and continually spun in the direction of the latest tremor. Still, he would not order the orbs to cut open the walls; he feared the consequences of letting his prisoners escape more then he feared the storm.

Asio sat atop the mushroom while the rest of the owls surrounded it. They had long since completely wrapped their departed king in his silk bedding and placed him under the mushroom's cap, guarding his body against the voracious spiders.

"What's happening, Asio? I'm scared," Calliope trilled.

"I don't know, but whatever it is, it's doing something to them," she replied. "We can't stay in here much longer. Hold steady, owls." Asio waited for a moment when the spiders were completely distracted -- if she could surprise them, they might have a chance to break out. But no matter what happened outside, there were always spiders watching them, and Asio knew the spiders would instantly forget their fear and kill them if they tried to cut their way out; they were outnumbered at least three-to-one, and she did not want to lead her people to a slaughter. To make matters worse, the tumult from the storm crazed the spiders, and their behavior became more and more erratic; at any moment they could swarm the owls and kill them anyway. Time was running out.

"What are we gonna do?" Calliope clicked her beak.

Asio closed her eyes, and in a solemn and quiet voice, spoke: "Otus, I know you are watching over us right now. I beseech you, come to our aid, we are in our darkest hour. We need you. I need you." A tear passed from her eye. At that moment, a meteor crashed into the webbed roof of the amphitheater and obliterated it, sending a shower of flaming rubble on those below. The spiders instantly freaked and scattered.

"Now owls, go! Take to the sky!" Asio cried. The owls spread their wings and bolted for the opening, their talons slicing apart any spider unfortunate enough to be in their way. Asio looked down at two remaining owls. "Loki, Wyeth, guard my husband. Let nothing happen to him."

"With our lives!" Loki replied.

Asio took off and spotted her target attempting to escape, running up the wall. Dodging fiery debris, Asio swooped in and without breaking stride, decapitated Ulric, his head dropping to the ground while his body kept moving.

"That's for Otus!"

She flew out of the prison, joining the other owls in freedom.

Glenna paced the throne room in a fit of tremulous rage. Compounding her fearful fury was the fact that the palace felt as though it would break apart at any minute from the constant quaking. Her mind raced in its fear. Why did she ever think Cornish was strong enough for this? He could barely perform a parlor trick before she came along. If she were the one with the ancestral blood, she would have been able to harness the power of the Maelstrom, except *she* would have bent the beast to her will. She ceased wallowing in her phantasmagoric delusions when the doors to the stately hall tore free of their moorings and blew open. In dashed her son. She couldn't bring herself to look upon the monstrosity in front of her; his appearance severed the last motherly fiber in her being and she felt nothing but revulsion.

"Dartmoor! What has happened to you?"

"Never mind that now! I have the Moonstone, Glenna. Where is the crown?"

"Your father has it, down in the dungeon."

"Father…" Dartmoor scowled, "get on!" He advanced on her and offered his diseased hand, which had strips of graying flesh dangling from it. She grasped his clammy, pestilent wrist with a squish, and a wave of nausea overtook her. He hoisted her onto the spider, and they whisked away.

Though the ground shook and the sky was filled with fire, the spiders focused on Pooka. They had heard about the power contained in this Spriggin's drum, and it was the only thing keeping them from swarming their prey. If he struck, they would all be dead and their queen in danger. They circled their quarry, hoping the tension would force a mistake. The deer had begun moving slowly toward the palace barricade without breaking formation. Dandelion and Ash sat motionless on their rides while Vivi growled at their adversaries. Fergus had long since taken cover deep within Dandelion's cloak, all three lightning bugs not far behind him.

Oscar sat perched on Hart's hindquarters. "Maybe I can make it," he said, looking to the balcony.

"No," Hart countered, "any sudden movement and they'll strike."

"We're running out of time!"

No one knew that better than Pooka. Annwyn no longer seemed to be living, the occasional raspy breath escaping her mouth the only sign of life. "Oscar," he whispered, "I want you to fly as fast as you can when I hit my drum."

"But that's suicide! The spiders'll be all over you in an instant!"

"I'll risk it. You're the only one of us who can get into that palace. Our only hope is the Moonstone."

Oscar's anxious look disappeared, and a smile broadened across his face: "No, that's not our only hope. Pooka, hit it NOW!"

The Owl King leapt into the air, and the spiders pounced. But the concussive force of Pooka's drum blasted them backwards. Suddenly, the sky filled with owls, swooping down and shredding to ribbons the arachnid aggressors under a cacophony of hoots and trills. The few remaining guards tried to escape, but they quickly met the same fate as the others. "Good to see you guys again!" Oscar hooted. The owls were elated to see their king alive, and they sang with joy.

"Into the palace!" Pooka shouted.

"Allow me!" Hart bellowed.

"Oh no, not again!!!" Ash clung to Hart for dear life and Vivi jumped clear. The buck reared up and charged the webbed portcullis, and with his mighty antlers, tore through it. Ama and the other deer followed, and the contingent of owls was close behind. The deer halted at the main entrance, and the owls circled overhead.

"This is as far as we can take you, good speed, friends," Ama said.

She and the other deer lowered themselves, and their passengers got down, Pooka with Annwyn in his arms. Thunder rumbled, and the winds whipped violently, shaking the ground and knocking them all off balance. It was at that moment they witnessed the most horrible thing they would ever know. In the blackening sky above the palace, the vortex split even further apart and tiny funnels formed on the rim, spinning so feverishly that they solidified into hundreds of teeth. The blazing clouds swirled around the mouth, congealing and morphing into a visage that would give demons nightmares. Once the sky birthed the monster's head, its mouth opened like the gateway to the underworld and split the heavens with a primeval shriek. Black eyes now formed out of the nebula and fixed on them.

"So this is how it ends," Dandelion said absentmindedly.

Pooka's voice cut through the din: "Inside! NOW!"

With Annwyn in his arms, he charged the palace, kicking in the door and rushing inside. Dandelion, Ash and Vivi followed with Oscar and the owls directly behind them.

Rage consumed Cornish at the sight of his prisoners daring to escape; his darkest and most macabre urges ran wild, making him salivate at the thought of the exquisite torture they deserved: "I will flay you, one at a time! There is no end to the pain you will suffer!"

"You're wearing the crown!" Oden seethed, the threats from Cornish deflected by rage. He couldn't believe what he was seeing. None of them could; it was blasphemy.

"What of it?"

"You're not even fit to look at the crown, filth!"

Llangollen pushed to the front of the prisoners and brandished the proboscis. "You killed the Owl King, didn't you? You forced my daughter into exile. You've destroyed countless lives and for what? So you could play dress-up and pretend to be king. You make me sick! I may die here today, but I will take you with me!"

"Ha! If only you were capable of such meager heroics!" Cornish waved his hand, expecting Llangollen's body to act in kind. But when nothing happened, genuine fear crossed his face.

"That's right, Nettle. We found your little minion; you won't be hurting me any more!" Llangollen and the others advanced on Cornish, who had dropped behind a phalanx of spiders.

"Kill them!" he yelled, falling back to the exit. The spiders attacked, but the owls dispatched the first of them, forcing the others to fall back and reconsider their strategy against such powerful fighters.

"Come back and fight, coward!" Llangollen roared.

Cornish nearly made it out when Dartmoor and Glenna bounded

into the chamber. Dartmoor produced the nacreous stone from the folds of his cloak and triumphantly held it aloft. "Father, I have the Moonstone!"

"Give it to me!" Unfazed by the boy's appearance, Cornish snapped it from his son so violently that the spider-mount bucked, knocking both Dartmoor and Glenna to the ground. Dartmoor gained his footing and backed away from his father while his mother took cover in one of the open cells.

Cornish turned back to the prisoners being held at bay by the spiders. "So you want a fight do you? Then you will have one. Pray for a quick death!" He inserted the Moonstone into the crown.

Instantly, the entire palace rumbled and swayed; a current of energy flowed through Cornish, and arcs of buzzing electricity jumped across his body. The stygian aura billowing from the crown pulsed around him, swathing him in shadow. He walked to the center of the chamber amid the spiders.

"Now you will witness true power!" He raised his arms, and the dark energy swirling around him grew in intensity. Everything went silent momentarily, and then he focused the power into a pillar of darkness he thrust into the ceiling, obliterating a considerable portion of the palace above their heads and leaving them exposed to the violent sky and the hellish form of the Maelstrom descending from above. The explosion flung everyone to the ground with such force that several spiders' bodies burst; yet Cornish remained standing.

"Only now, at the end, do you realize the futility of opposing me! Prepare to meet your doom!"

"I don't think so!"

"You!" Dartmoor wheezed.

Cornish spun around, and there, in the entrance, was Oscar at the head of a legion of owls. "Ha! I should have known that you would have been foolish enough to return here, *Owl King*! You are too late, I have already won. The crown is mine!"

"We'll see about that. NOW!" Oscar shouted, and the full flock of owls swept into the chamber, engaging the spiders in combat. The spiders met them mid-air, foes trading fangs and talons. The Spriggin prisoners backed away from the melee, gravitating to the far wall.

"Our liege has returned! We must help him! Take wing!" Oden commanded, and Oakley, Ludwig and Sadé joined their kin in battle. The spiders were quick, but they were quickly being overrun by the fleet and ferocious owls. Vivi, once again sporting Fergus, ran into the chamber and entered the fray, nipping and tearing legs in a mad dash. Ash and Dandelion charged behind, and the newly emboldened Flicker Brothers buzzed in and flashed their bottoms.

"Dandelion!" Verbena yelled. Dandelion caught sight of her family, and she and Ash braved the battle to join their parents for a tearful, if fearful, reunion.

Cornish stood in the middle of it all, his dark power surging, barely fazed by the bedlam around him. He held his arm out, and the evil energy swarmed over it, elongating and forming a lance. He swung his weapon, and it stretched to an incredible length. Almost too fast for the eye to follow, Cornish swatted owls out of the air like flies. He focused on Oscar and attempted to impale him, but the Owl King proved too deft a flyer to bring down, even with the missing tail feathers. Meanwhile, the massive jaws of the Maelstrom descended ever closer, drawn to the evil in Cornish. The beast opened its mouth and inhaled, creating a vacuum which began to draw everything to it.

It was then that Pooka appeared in the archway holding Annwyn.

"Oh no! Annwyn! My baby!" Gwilyn choked.

Cornish retracted his lance and leveled his fury at Pooka and Annwyn. He drew back his arm to strike. The winded Pooka didn't have a chance; he gripped Annwyn and closed his eyes, waiting for annihilation.

"Ha! I'll enjoy this! Make peace with your gods—AHHHH!"

Cornish's weapon began its death-dealing descent, but instead of striking the slumping Spriggins, the energy lance swung wildly about the dungeon, rending apart walls and slicing open the chamber housing Erebus. In his flailing, the crown flew from his head and landed with a loud clanking on the floor. Cornish collapsed. Instantly, the dark energy he wielded dissipated, and yet the Maelstrom still came for them, the sucking winds growing stronger by the moment.

Behind him stood Llangollen, the proboscis in his right hand, dripping blood. "That's for my daughter," he spat.

Oscar saw the crown hit the floor, and swooped down, grasping it in his talons. He landed next to Pooka and put it on. In contrast to Cornish, Oscar took an ethereal glow, the opaline stone combining with the other gems in the crown to produce an intertwining aura of colors. He leaned down and touched Annwyn's forehead with the Moonstone, prismatic tendrils enveloping her; the Emerald Flower, which had been dormant since the stabbing, flared to life and interacted with the crown, adding green to the swirling energies. Annwyn flinched and then opened her eyes.

"Annwyn, you're alive!" Oscar cried. Pooka hugged her even closer to his chest.

Annwyn did not speak at first, but her eyes widened and she pointed to the sky, "Look," she managed, her thin voice barely audible.

The Maelstrom opened its mouth and a twister formed, creeping toward them like an eager tongue. It came for them, snaring trees, houses, stones and anything else in its path, delivering them into the monstrosity's gullet. In a few moments, it would devour them before turning its wrath on the rest of Anglia.

"What was it Ismene said?" Oscar frantically trilled. "What are we supposed to do?"

"The ring," Annwyn whispered, barely conscious, "the ring and the Moonstone."

She lacked the strength to move, but Pooka knew what to do. He lifted Annwyn's arm for her and touched the Emerald Flower to Oscar's bowed head. The energies surrounding them refocused and blasted forth, directly into the twister-tongue, reversing its rotation and sending it back toward the gaping mouth of the Maelstrom. The beast thrashed in resistance, threatening to rend the sky asunder, but it could not overcome the combined might of the fabled ring and legendary stone. Their righteous power forced the twister deep into the Maelstrom's head, and it continued spinning faster and faster until its demonic visage trembled and tore apart, exploding with a concussive force that shook the land. The floating remnants of the creature in the sky were quickly slurped up by the vortex before it collapsed on itself, leaving nothing behind.

"We did it!" Oscar cheered. "Ha, ha!"

"Annwyn," Pooka spoke softly and kissed her forehead.

"This isn't over yet!" Cornish fought to regain his footing, hand clutching his side in an attempt to staunch the bleeding. He drew a blade from within his robes. "I will still see you dead, Owl King! Ahhh!" He staggered forward, sword held high.

Oscar rose to meet his challenger, but before he could reach him, a gargantuan black widow spider crawled from out of the wreckage -- Erebus. The Owl King returned to Annwyn's side should he need the ring's power, but Erebus was not there for them. She was there for the one who plotted her overthrow and forced her to feed on her children. She was there for the one who kept her imprisoned and drained her of her juices. She was there for Cornish. She spied her prey and fell upon him quickly. Not even leaving him time to scream, she pulled the Spriggin to her mouth and plunged her fangs into him; it was as if he had the air sucked out of his body while she fed. Glenna let out a piercing scream when the spider tossed her husband's husk to the floor. Erebus turned her ebony stare on the gorgon and her cowering son. "No! Take him! NOOO!!!"

With incredible speed, Erebus seized Glenna and encased her in a silk cocoon, muffling her screeching. Dartmoor wailed and fled from the grotesque spider, shoving his way out of the dungeon and emitting a feral braying. The Queen held her next meal in her fangs and scurried out of the wreckage and into the woods, a wave of darkness leaving with her.

The owls and Spriggins slowly got up and looked around.

"Is it over?" Perry asked.

Verbena picked up her son and kissed him. "Yes sweetie, it is."

Annwyn opened her eyes briefly and looked lovingly upon her

savior. "Pooka-bear . . ."

She smiled, kissed his cheek, and passed out.

CHAPTER 11

A Farewell and a New Beginning

Otus's body lay in state, wrapped in a shroud upon a mushroom pedestal in the center of the Fairy Circle for mourners to pay their final respects. The owls had gathered around Oscar, who gently held his mother as they stoically watched over the departed king. The entire Spriggin village began their procession into the circle, led by Annwyn and her family. She wore a stunning white dress flecked with a verdant hue from the Emerald Flower, which gave off an iridescent glow, in addition to a pair of radiant swallowtail wings, a replacement for her old pair long lost to the woods. None of the Spriggins were without their wings, and they all opened and closed them slowly in deference to the occasion. Pooka, Ash and Dandelion flanked Annwyn, their families assembled around them as well. The forest fairies filed into the amphitheater and took their seats. Quite dramatically, Emmlen, now resplendent in a beautiful, flowing azure gown, entered the circle amid hushed whispers and incredulous stares, accompanied by Flax, Fern, Fein and several other water fairies. To most of the attendees, she was known only in myth, a story of such fantastic and epic proportions it just couldn't be true, but lo, here she was among them. The majesty and elegance of her appearance, coupled with Oscar's approving nod, quelled any nascent anxiety, and she was accorded a place of respect close to the pedestal as befitting her station.

All of the woodland animals also congregated there to bid farewell to Otus: Fergus, Phineas and the frogs; the foxes, including Vivi; Hart, Ama, Grace and the rest of the herd; the badgers, beavers, birds, bugs and of course, Riley Rumplefeather, who found himself in the one scenario where even he would agree that keeping his mouth shut was a good idea. Ellie sat under a mushroom umbrella for shade, the curious shape of Ismene attached to her shell. Even the worms wriggled up out of the soil and found the most advantageous spot to watch the ceremony. And hovering in the forefront of the circle were the Flicker Brothers, their bottoms emitting a muted light befitting the mood.

Annwyn and Oscar took their places at the moss podium; Annwyn had been chosen to represent the Spriggins on this day for her bravery and heroics in stopping the Maelstrom. Annwyn and Oscar looked at each other, still in weary disbelief about all that had recently transpired. The Owl King stepped forward, the crown a dazzling, luminous sight. Any hushed conversations instantly ceased.

"We are gathered here today to say farewell to a great ruler and a great owl, my father, Otus, who, in this grave time, fell defending his peoples. He will be missed by all who knew him and all who live in Anglia Forest, but he would not want any more sorrow to fill our hearts. We have carried a heavy burden for long enough. It is a mournful day, but it is also a day for great joy. We have rid the land of a terrible evil and forged new alliances that will most surely endure for generations." He bowed at Emmlen, who returned the gesture. "So take heart! Feel the sun's rays on your faces once again, smell the fresh air laden with honeydew. This is a day to celebrate the return of peace and tranquility to Anglia. Now we lay to rest King Otus, may his spirit ever be with us."

Annwyn began to play her flute, the solemn notes carrying a delicate and wistful song throughout the entire forest. Loki and Wyeth gently lifted Otus's body and flew it to its final resting spot: a newly built sepulcher centered in the mushroom circle at the heart of Willow Hills. Led by Oscar and Asio, all of them filed out of the Fairy Circle in a somber procession, Annwyn accompanying it with the melody. They marched through the village, the extensive damage and smoldering wreckage a reminder of their pyrrhic victory. They reached the site, and the two owls flew Otus inside, laying him to rest in the tomb. They emerged, and Asio fell to the ground, sorrowfully saying her final goodbyes. Oscar comforted his mother, the Moonstone blazing forth from the crown. Those who had held their grief inside now let it out, sobbing and moaning.

Ismene and Ellie stepped forward before the gathering. The little mushroom allowed more time for their sadness before clearing his throat. "Inhabitants of Anglia, many of you do not know me. I am but a humble fellow who has spent ages watching the forest. In my time, I have seen many great beings come and go, but none so valiant as Otus. Remember that as old forms pass away, it may be tempting to give in to the pang in our heats and dwell on our loss. Do not allow it to be so. Otus may have left our world, but he has ascended to another, and will continue to watch over us, as he has always done. Even the plants teach us this lesson: As one dies, the Earth readies for a new one to take its place and continue life. So shall we all see the end of our days, so shall we see the beginnings of new ones. It is our time to carry on and live by the ideals our departed friend championed. Let us cherish our time together. To Otus."

"To Otus," the crowd replied in unison.

Annwyn resumed playing her flute, but now with a more vivid tune, encouraging the tears to fade away and reminding the mourners of better times with the King.

Asio rose from the ground, wiped her face, and hugged her son. "Your father would be so proud of you," she smiled through her tears.

"I know he would," he replied, hugging her tightly. Oscar felt the warmth of a sudden sunbeam spread across his face, so he looked up, and there, perched on the canopy, was his father, who effused a noble aura that shone brighter than a thousand suns. Otus gazed upon his son for a moment, smiled, and then flew off to join his fathers in the sky.

The ceremony over, the congregation made their way back down to the Fairy Circle for the final benedictions. Amid the crowds funneling back into the amphitheater, Annwyn looked around and noticed it was a tremendous day, like early spring after a long and bitter winter; everything was so lush and vivid, and the pleasant fragrances of honeysuckle and lavender filled the air. Tiny, happy, purple forget-me-nots lined the paths while radiant, red trumpet vines called the attention of the crowd to Annwyn and Oscar as they entered the Fairy Circle and resumed their places on the dais.

The crowd hushed when Emmlen strode forth, flanked by her retinue, and stood before them. "Beings of the Known Realms, I give you King Oscar and Queen Annwyn, rulers of all of Anglia Forest." A startled murmur rolled through the audience

"Queen? I'm no queen! How could this be?"

Ellie, with Ismene on her back, trundled over to Emmlen. "It's quite simple, really," the mushroom said. "You wear the Emerald Flower, heirloom of Olwynn Bluebell, once the Queen of Anglia. By using that ring with the Moonstone, you were able to destroy the Maelstrom, and thus, fulfill the prophecy. See? Simple."

"What he says is true," Emmlen proclaimed. "Thanks to Annwyn Bluebell, the fogs have lifted from the Emerald Lake, and the waters have been restored to a beautiful blue. My palace has risen from the depths to take its rightful place on the surface, and the Hall of Heroes has its final statue. I am once again Emmlen, Lady of Azuria. Only the one chosen by the Fates would have been able to complete such momentous tasks, and here she is before us, Annwyn Bluebell, Queen of Anglia!"

The crowd roared in approval. Annwyn stood dazed for a moment. Oscar looked to her, put his wing around her and moved in.

"Whew, I hope this doesn't mean we're married."

They hugged each other as everyone filled the amphitheater with cries of happiness and sounds of glee. The deer bowed their heads, Fergus and Phineas leapt into the air, and Vivi howled. The lightning bugs flashed with excitement, and Rumplefeather finally had an excuse to make as much noise as he wanted.

Oscar raised a wing to call the throng to order, and they complied. "Well, your highness, it's only fitting you address your new subjects. What say all of you? Will you hear your queen speak?"

The crowd whooped and hollered with calls for a speech.

There they were; the creepy crawlies squirmed in Annwyn's stomach again.

"Oscar, what are you doing?"

"Sorry, your majesty. The people have spoken."

Annwyn stepped forward, and the gathered masses quieted down in anticipation.

"I really don't know what to say. It's almost too much to take in…I pledge I will never betray your trust, and Oscar and I will do all we can to make sure our land never falls into darkness again. We have a lot of work to do to rebuild our lives, but I know there's nothing in this world that can stop us if we work together. So, from this moment forth, let us begin to heal our wounds and usher in a new day. Long live Anglia!"

The assembly greeted these words with a hearty cheer.

Taking this as his cue, Pooka thumped his drum, the driving beat quickly complimented by the trumpet vines. Ash joined in on his mandolin, and coupled with Dandelion's tambourine, the rest of the orchestra took up the rollicking music; a party was now in full swing, and it spilled out of the Fairy Circle and into the surrounding woods.

Life was everywhere again, and the entire forest hummed with energy. Annwyn could not remember a time when everything in the forest looked so green. Everyone was having a wonderful time, dancing, singing, tasting nectar wine, forgetting all their worries. Joy was bountiful. Butterflies, moths and bees buzzed, dove and swooped in the air around and throughout the village. Chickadees sat perched on the trumpet vines and sang in tune, while the crows and jays cawed from above, filling the forest with their songs. Dandelion and Ash left the orchestra and began to dance alongside the other Spriggins already filling the Fairy Circle with many kinds of jigs and flutters. Much to everyone's delight, the Spriggins spontaneously took to the air and continued their revelry. With the return of the Moonstone and the Emerald Flower, the Spriggins were able to use their wings all the time, not solely during the full moon.

"This is great!" Dandelion enthused, high above the ground. Ash dipped her, then twirled her around. She laughed till her stomach was sore, and he joined in.

Gwilyn watched Dandelion and Ash then turned to her husband. "Would you care to dance, my love?" He answered by grabbing his wife by the waist and leading her to the center of the circle, where they delighted in dancing about. Abe and Calysta Alder, Scarlet and Thurston Rose, and Poppy and Verbena Buttercup joined them, though they danced at a slightly lower altitude than their high-flying children.

"I'm so glad everything has returned to normal. Well, as normal as it can be when your little girl suddenly becomes queen!" Llangollen laughed, and he dipped Gwilyn back. "I have missed this."

"I've missed you," Gwilyn cooed, hugging her husband. "Our family is complete again. We're complete again."

Abe danced around the group in a rare display of excitement, startling the others with his herky-jerky and unpracticed shimmying and gamboling. After all they had been through, Abe's dancing was a rarified bit of boogying indeed if it could cause such a stir. "Yee-hah! I knew the kids'd come through, a chip off the ol' block that Ash is!"

"He must take after me then," Calysta chided him. They all laughed, even the crimson-faced Abe.

"They were raised right," Verbena beamed with pride.

"Yes, yes they were," Thurston said, hugging Scarlet.

Annwyn and Oscar stood before the merriment, and it pleased their hearts to see everyone in such high spirits. The line to greet the new King and Queen grew, as everyone wanted to congratulate and thank them for their unwavering strength and hope, much to the embarrassment of the humble Sprig and the delight of the bold Owl King. The well wishers in the queue stepped aside to allow Emmlen and her courtiers to genuflect before Oscar and Annwyn. The beautiful water fairy rose.

"I am glad to see both of you in far better spirits than when we were last together. You have succeeded where others would have surely failed. But because you have prevailed, Anglia will know true harmony once again. Thank you." She leaned over, kissed them both on their foreheads, and bowed. Fein, Fern and Flax lowered their heads in gratitude.

"I had faith in you all along," Fern whispered as they turned and took their leave of the new monarchs.

"You have saved us," said an aged Spriggin, bowing before the nobles. "Thank you!"

"The bards will weave a new tale from your deeds, one that will stand alongside the greatest legends of Anglia and beyond!" yet another Spriggin gushed.

Again and again, admirers showered them with accolades, yet Annwyn and Oscar felt awkward accepting all the praise, for many had struggled and sacrificed to defeat the evil, and they vowed, then and there, to honor them with a monument so their heroism would not go unsung. Annwyn was bowing to acknowledge the latest laudation when she lifted her head to behold, standing before her, the most welcome sight she had ever seen. It was Pooka. Her eyes widened, and her heart pounded.

"There's something I've been meaning to tell you," she said.

Before he could respond, she took his hand and pulled him close. Their lips met in a long and passionate kiss. A roar of applause erupted and poured forth from the crowd.

They pulled apart, and Pooka looked deeply into her eyes: "I've always wanted to tell you the same thing."

They turned and faced the cheering masses. Peace had returned to Anglia Forest, and it filled the hearts of everyone joined together in harmony to celebrate the beginning of a new age.